The Rose Contingency

This novel's story and characters are fictitious. Certain existing institutions, companies, and locations are mentioned, but the characters involved and their interactions therewith are wholly imaginary.

ISBN: 9798781541393

"This is the way the world ends.
Not with a bang but a whimper."

-T. S. Eliot, The Hollow Men

PROLOGUE

My name is Alexander Lee, and I am the last human on earth.

Before I say anything else, you need to truly understand what you are holding in your hands. This is more than just a memoir or a diary. This is the answer to the questions you haven't yet thought to ask. This is the record of the path that led to you. This is the final chapter in the story of the modern world. This story was not easy to live, and I'm guessing it won't be easy to read either.

Though everything recounted here happened over the course of the last few weeks, it seems like a lifetime since anything was normal. Currently, I spend my days alternating between working and writing. I don't sleep much, so sometimes that's how I spend my nights as well. I'm sure you're probably confused and a little disoriented, wondering who you are, and maybe even why you are. I will do my best to explain, but honestly I don't know if words on a page will ever really be enough.

The world as it is to your understanding is full of life, energy, and activity. But as you step out the door into the world as it exists now, you will find it very different. There is an emptiness there now that I can't really explain. It's something you will have to experience for yourself. Fortunately, you won't have to be alone the way that I have been. I made sure of that.

I have to admit I don't really know exactly how to tell this story. It's all still so fresh and I'm not really a storyteller. But given the circumstances, I don't really think that I have a choice.

So, here goes.

The world as we knew it ended in the year 2032. Suffice it to say that it didn't really go the way that we all thought it would. There were no zombies or alien invaders. In fact, much of the world didn't even realize it was happening until it was too late.

I guess before we get too far in to all that, let's start with a little backstory.

My full name is Alexander Hamilton Lee. You can save any comments on my first and middle name combo, I've heard them all. Yes, he was one of the founding fathers of our country and yes, I know that he was never actually president. Also, my name has nothing to do with the musical from several years ago. Basically he was the first Secretary of the Treasury of the United States. He was also the father of the country's financial system and the founder of the US Coast Guard. Oh, and he used to be on the ten dollar bill.

More relevantly, he was the founder of The New York Post, which is why he was my namesake. My dad works at The Post.

He *worked* at The Post, up until a few weeks ago. He was a reporter for years and then he transferred to layout as he got older and the field work got to be a little too much for him. I grew up in Wichita Falls, Texas with my parents and my sister, Shayra.

She's pretty important to this story as well. Shayra Rose Lee was the greatest scientific mind of our generation. And I'm the last human on the planet so that is the official word on the subject. When you read this, make sure that goes into the annals of history. That is, if those are actually a real thing and if they still exist somewhere.

I'm not sure where my parents got Shayra's first name from, but you can thank the movie *Titanic* for her middle name. It came out a few months before she was born. I love my parents, but I think it's safe to say they weren't very creative when it came to naming children.

I still can't believe they're really gone. And Shayra too. When I would imagine apocalypse scenarios and watch zombie movies when I was younger, it was always the faceless, generic people who were part of the body count. I never imagined having to watch the people I loved die in real life. But I did.

Sorry. Like I said, it's all still pretty fresh. Death, you will learn, is just a part of life. And it's the worst part.

So my dad worked at the Times Record News in Wichita Falls until he got his dream job at The Post about fifteen years ago. I'm still not sure if Alexander Hamilton was my dad's hero because he founded The Post, or if my dad wanted to work at The Post because he loved Hamilton.

I guess it doesn't really matter now. Especially not to you.

After he got the job, he was able to work remotely for about five years, but at that point they insisted that he move to New York. My dad loved Wichita Falls, as did the rest of us, but when it looked like he might lose the job if he didn't move, we knew he had to go. He had named his only son after the founder of the paper, so it was obviously important to him.

So, my parents moved to New York and Shayra, who was just out of OSU on a chemistry degree, decided to move to Fort Worth to intern with a company called Lykos Biotech, a small but successful lab specializing in biochemistry. At least that's what she told me. At the time, I had no idea what that meant.

So, being the needy man-child that I am, and not wanting to be alone, I decided to move with Shayra to Fort Worth. I think she mostly agreed to get an apartment together to save on rent. The internship with Lykos paid, but not much. But, if I'm honest, I think she was also secretly happy to have somebody to take care of. She was always that kind of big sister. She always had an extra twenty dollar bill in her purse in case I forgot to bring my money to the mall.

God, I miss her.

I'm sure you are familiar with what they call "survivor's guilt." If not, let me explain. It's where somebody survives some sort of disaster or tragedy even though other people didn't and the survivor is left with an overwhelming sense of guilt for still being alive. If I'm honest, I've always thought that was kind of silly. Why feel guilty? It's simple luck of the draw, as are so many things in life. You happened to survive and were given a chance to live the rest of your life. Feeling bad won't give the people who didn't survive that same chance. So, who are you really helping?

But I think I get it now. Imagine surviving a disaster that didn't just kill a bunch of people, but literally everybody. And I don't mean literally in the overused, over exaggerated way that they did in the 2010s. I mean *literally* literally.

Why do I find myself with such guilt over being the last human? One would assume it's because I've experienced an unimaginable trauma that the human mind was never built to handle.

I wish it was that simple.

So what happened to everyone else? With such advanced technology, medicine, and military power, how did the human race fall so quickly and completely? Unfortunately there was no amount of military strength that could abate this particular threat. What good are guns against an enemy you can't even see? And as for technology and medicine, let's just say our best efforts were unsuccessful.

After reading the account contained in these pages, you may find it tempting to call me a hero. But I would strongly advise against that. Yes, I fought, I sacrificed, and I gave all that I could to make sure the events of my time were a semicolon in the story of mankind, rather than a full stop. A new chapter, instead of an ending. But I think that anyone in my position would have done the same. To call that a heroic act would be setting the bar far too low. But that's not the only reason I say that I didn't earn the title of hero. In fact, I didn't really earn any of this.

I could sit here and reflect on the question of why I alone survived out of all of the talented, deserving, and beautiful people that made up the human race in the year 2032. I could summarize everything that happened and draw a concise line back to the root cause of all this. But I can't.

Don't get me wrong, I am deeply acquainted with the answers to all of those questions. And once you've finished reading this account, you will be too. However, circumventing the path that led us here won't do the story justice.

You won't find this story anywhere in the information you initially received. You won't find it in world history or anywhere on what remains of the internet. In fact, I wish it was a story that you didn't have to be told at all. And it is the height of cruel irony that I have to be the one to tell it.

See, that's the thing about survivors guilt, I always saw it as this imagined thing. A purely psychological way for your brain to deal with a tragic situation. But not this time.

You see, there's one important detail that I haven't told you yet. It's the horrible truth I have to live with. It's the reason I don't sleep much. The story you now hold in your hands, the story of the fall of mankind and the death of every human on the planet, save one, can be summed up into one devastating statement.

It was all my fault.

1

Friday, April 16th, 2032

I sat in Roger Kingston's office at Masterson Paper and Packaging with a familiar sinking feeling in my stomach. Being called into the boss's office was not exactly a new experience, but the unsettling feeling that accompanied it never wained in potency.

What had I done this time? I quickly riffled through my memories from the last couple of weeks. Was this about the fact that I missed my scheduled dock time at the Fitzburg warehouse? Surely not. I had made the delivery up the next day and they weren't even mad. Or because I went and gave blood on Tuesday without asking? I had done it at lunch and it barely took more than an hour, so I couldn't see him being upset about that. Maybe it was because of the two hour lunch I took on Monday. I was up far too late the night before and I had fallen asleep on the couch when I went home for lunch. Stupid YouTube.

No. No, there's no way they could know about that. Maybe it was because I got into a bit of a disagreement with Carl, the warehouse manager, yesterday. Yes, that had to be it. Carl was not the kind of guy to let something like that go without tattling.

Dang it, Carl.

Roger was the operations manager, which made him Carl's boss. He sat on the front edge of his large mahogany desk. I say mahogany because it looked fancy, not because I actually know how to tell the difference in types of wood. He was cleaning his glasses with a small black cloth that he kept in his desk drawer at all times. He was not really the kind of man who would use his shirt to clean his glasses. For one, his blue dress shirt was tucked firmly into his black dress pants. For two, it was stiff from being overly starched. It was made out of a thick, uncomfortable looking material. It was clearly cheap but made to look expensive. In my opinion, that summed Roger up pretty well.

"Listen Alex," he started without looking up from the thorough cleaning job that was happening in his hands, "we need to talk."

"I agree, that's why I called this meeting," I quipped, trying to cut the heaviness in the room.

His thumb stopped mid-circle on the lens of his glasses. He moved his head up just enough that he could bring his eyes the rest of the way to meet my gaze. The menacing quality this gave his stare made it inescapably clear that he did not find my sarcasm amusing.

The depth of his solemnity surprised me. This was not the first run-in I'd had with Carl in the eight months I had worked here. Roger knew he was a jerk and prone to power trips, so he never took his complaints all that seriously. He would usually call me in and give me the obligatory rant about respect and "chain of command" and whatever else fit with that particular infraction. Then he would usually end with something passive-aggressive like "I know he can be difficult, but you'll find that the drivers who do their job well don't usually have much trouble with him." Then he'd chuckle because he found himself oh-so-clever. There was no such levity today.

"Here's the thing," he continued without breaking eye contact, "I think we've been incredibly patient with you."

He raised his glasses to rest on his face and adjusted the bridge slightly so that it rested midway on his nose. As he did, the corner of his mouth curled slightly into a barely noticeable smirk.

The levity I was looking for? No. I knew that smirk. The same smirk I had seen on his face when he informed everybody that there would be no Christmas bonuses for anyone except upper management. Roger was a bit of a sadist, and that smirk usually meant he was about to do something that would cause somebody else a considerable amount of pain.

Crap.

"But there comes a time when patience runs out. Before I go any further, do you have anything you need to tell me about Monday?"

"Uh…Nope," I lied.

"So I'm guessing you didn't know that we had GPS trackers installed in all the trucks last Thursday?"

Double crap.

"Whuh…" Some combination of "what" and "uh-oh" was about all that I could manage.

"It seems your truck was parked outside your apartment building for two hours and seven minutes on

Monday around lunch time. Now, I double checked your manifest to see if *maybe* you had a couple of deliveries at that address," he was enjoying this way too much, "but sadly I didn't see anything. As it turns out, you just had yourself a nice long lunch."

"Ok, see…I didn't mean…it was…" I don't know why I tried to explain. I knew it wouldn't work. "You see…YouTube."

"Look, there are dozens of people lined up who would kill for a job like this."

"I don't feel like that's accurate," I muttered under my breath.

"What?"

"Nothing."

He furrowed his brow and let out what seemed to me at the time to be the longest exasperated sigh in human history.

"The bottom line is we just don't have a place at this company for somebody who is that careless with company time."

"Look Rog- Uh…Mr. Kingston, sir. It was a total accident! I fell asleep on the couch because…you remember Justin Bieber? Well he hosts this YouTube show about celebrities pranking people in nursing homes—"

"Oh good grief!" he interrupted impatiently. "I don't really care what the show is about. Look, it's not just about Monday. It seems like every week it's something with you. In fact, just this morning Carl was telling me that you missed your dock time at Fitzburg last week, and yesterday he said you spoke to him in an extremely disrespectful manner when he asked you to sweep the warehouse."

DANG IT, CARL.

"I know. I'm sorry. Please, Mr. Kingston. I need this job so bad."

"No more chances, Alex. You're done."

The finality in those words made my heart drop. He reached his hand out right in front of my nose.

"Give me your key card and go clock out."

I slammed the door of my 2003 Sentra so hard, I was hoping Roger heard it. Or felt it. In his face. How could he be so heartless? I practically begged him and he wouldn't even consider giving me another chance.

The worst part was that I knew he had made the right decision. I would've fired me too. I would've fired me a couple of months ago when I crashed the forklift into those shelves and brought down three sections of product. I mean, I would've given myself a generous severance package, but I still would've fired me. Unfortunately, such things are not required by law in Texas so as of today my income stream had officially ended.

Shayra was going to be pissed. We'd had this conversation before. A couple of times. In fact, this was the third job I had been fired from in the last two years.

I closed my eyes, released a deep sigh of emotional exhaustion and let my head slowly come to rest on the top of the worn leather steering wheel.

Almost immediately I remembered that, even in April, the Texas heat can bring the interior trim of a car to scorching temperatures after just a few hours in the sun. My head instinctively recoiled from the source of the searing pain and I let out an involuntary grunt of pain that grew in to a growling crescendo of frustration.

I stretched my neck so that I could see my reflection in the rearview mirror. Already a bright red line was forming where my skin had rested on the steering wheel. I relaxed my body and collapsed unceremoniously back into my seat.

"Awesome," I grumbled sarcastically.

I inserted the key into the ignition and turned it to the start position. A whirring sound indicated that the starter mechanism had failed to engage again. The starter was going out. I knew that. It was one of the many things I had mentally filed away to deal with later. It was an irresponsibly long list by now.

Two more attempts and it worked. The four cylinder engine reluctantly sputtered to life and settled into a quiet purr. Quiet, except the repetitive clicking that indicated a valve lifter was sticking.

I reached down and put the the car in drive, burning my hand on the gear shift for good measure. After pulling forward out of the spot that I had backed into that morning, I began the forty-five minute commute home.

2

The drive home took less time than usual. I'm sure they didn't want to pay me for more hours than they had to, so Mr. Kingston called me into his office a few minutes after 3:00 p.m. Our meeting, though it had felt far longer, had only lasted about ten minutes. Between that and my time spent cooking my forehead in the car, I had pulled out of the parking lot about 3:30, leaving me with much less traffic to contend with than a 5:00 commute. By 3:45, I was passing Western Place, a pair of office buildings just before the Ridgmar exit off of I-30. Two identical nondescript beige rectangles reaching ten stories into the sky. I've never been in the west tower but as I understand it's mostly medical offices. A hospice, a pediatric home health service, etc.

The east tower contained, among other things, the headquarters for Lykos Biotech, which occupied the entire ninth and tenth floors. Shayra was fortunate enough to work so close to where we lived. I say fortunate, but the truth is that it couldn't have been more intentional. She had interned at Lykos for two years before they offered her a full time position. Although they told her several times that they would have offered her the position sooner, if it weren't for the fact that completing a two year internship before becoming a full fledged employee was "an unfortunate policy." My sister was good at what she did and everybody knew it. It's why they made her lead project manager on this big new project. The project that everyone in the lab wanted.

After she was made an official research associate, she bought a new car. A Prius hybrid. Because of the environment or something, she said. That shiny new car was enough to make her forget about the long commute for a time. But that only lasted about two years before she was ready to find a new living situation closer to work. So, we moved to the Ridgmar area. It was a nice little neighborhood on the west side of Fort Worth consisting of some houses, roughly a dozen apartment complexes, a large assortment of shops and restaurants lining the west side, and a country club crowning it to the north. Choosing an apartment in that neighborhood was the natural choice since Western Place was situated along I-30 at the southeast corner. Shayra often mentioned how she could see our apartment building from some of the windows at Lykos headquarters.

As I switched on my right turn signal to indicate my intent to exit at Ridgmar, I hoped she was too busy to look out of said windows and notice my car arriving home almost two hours earlier than normal. No need to have the terrible discussion that was forthcoming any sooner than absolutely necessary. With luck, I could find some job postings online and already have a few prospects ready in order to help sugar coat the awful truth of todays vocational failure. I accelerated slowly down the driveway of Renaissance Gardens Apartments after waiting for the metal gate to clamor to a stop in the open position. I was already preparing my defense for this evenings conversation.

I mean, it wasn't that great of a job anyway. In fact, if you think about it—

My car squeaked and squealed to a premature stop. Shayra's pristinely washed white Prius sat in her assigned parking space. She was already home.

If I hadn't seen her car, I wouldn't have known she was home upon entering the living room of our second floor apartment. My sister liked to work in the dark, and so she had insisted on blackout curtains on all of the living room windows. She sat in the recliner on the far side of the room with her silver laptop resting atop a gray fleece blanket that covered most of her body. The afternoon sun light from the front door washed over her face, betraying her presence in the otherwise unlit room. She had a bad habit of sitting in the dark and working on her computer, no matter how many times I told her it was bad for her eyes.

Her head shot up like a startled deer and she gazed at me inquisitively. Like always, her red hair was pulled back into a perfect pony tail, while a strand on each side remained hanging out in the front, framing her face. Her mouth curled downward into the slightest frown as she looked intently towards the door with unblinking eyes. Most likely because her eyes were already adjusted to the intensity of the harsh sunlight from the almost equally intense brightness of her screen that I had told her dozens of times was—

"You're home early," she said suspiciously.

"You're home…at all," I rebutted.

She often worked late and many times I was in bed long before she got home. And yet here she was, home before 4:00 p.m.

"Uh, yeah…" she shook her head, as if to release the quizzical fog, "…they uh, sent me home. Why are you here?"

"Same," I reached back and closed the door. "We got all the orders for Monday pulled early so they told me to take off."

That half truth seemed to satisfy her suspicion for the time being.

"Huh," she said acceptingly as her eyes returned to her computer screen, its pale illumination now the only source of light in the room.

I reached over and flipped the switch that powered a stand lamp in the corner of the room. I would protect her eyes even if she refused to.

"Why did they send you home?" I asked. "Is everything ok?"

Her eyes returned to me.

"Oh, yeah. They just said I've been working too much and should go home and get some rest. Well, the jokes on them because I can work from home!" She held one finger up in the air to signify her triumph over their oppressive behavior and then quickly turned her attention back to the screen.

"You've always worked too much. Why do they have a problem with it now?"

"I have a new round of experiments starting on Monday," she said, her eyes still fixed to the computer.

"What kind of experiments?"

"For the project."

"Ah, yes. The mysterious project." I made my way to the couch next to her chair and plopped down on the side nearest to where she sat. "The one you can't tell me anything about. How's that going?"

"Still can't tell you."

"You can't tell me anything?"

"Nope."

"Can you tell me the name of the project?"

"Project Nil."

"Really?" I said, genuinely surprised that she had shared that information. "Why do you call it that?"

She stopped typing and looked over at me with a smirk, "Because that's how much I can tell you about it."

She gave me a mischievous grin that wrinkled her freckled nose before she went back to her furious note taking or web searching or whatever it was that she was doing. I shook my head and let out an indignant chuckle.

"Ok, fine," I conceded. "You win this round."

"I win every round," she gloated.

As I stared straight ahead at the rarely used fireplace on the wall opposite from where I sat, my lingering smile from her joke began to fade. I had insisted that we pay extra for a unit with a fireplace, begged even. Yet, in the six years we had lived here we had used it a total of three times. All on Christmas day when our parents had come to visit. Since they lived so far away and neither Shayra and I, nor they wanted to make that trip every time, we decided to alternate each year as to who would traverse the country in the name of Christmas.

Three times we had used that fireplace. And yet every month our rent was higher because I had insisted on it. Because of my lapse in judgement.

How could I possibly tell her that I had been fired again? How could I look her in the eye and inform her that she was once again going to have to pay the price for my stupid decision?

I couldn't. And yet I had to.

"Shay…" I started.

"Yeah?" she said as she looked up.

Do it. Rip off the band-aid.

"I...am getting hungry. What do you want to do for dinner?"

Just tell her.

Her eyes shifted slightly to the clock in the corner of her screen.

"It's not even 4:00 yet," she observed.

"Uh, yeah, I didn't get to eat lunch."

"Oh. I guess I didn't either. Anything in particular sound good?"

"Maybe Asian food?" I asked.

Asian food and lies, you coward.

"Yeah, Asian sounds good. Little Saigon?"

"Sounds perfect."

"I'll go call it in," she said as she closed her computer and tossed the blanket aside, climbing out of the brown leather chair with an agility that didn't even begin to betray her age of almost thirty-four.

She stayed in fairly good shape and was one of the healthiest eaters I had ever met. She claimed it helped her stay focused on the more complex aspects of her work. Something about eating plenty of tyrosine and flavonoids. I had to look the second one up because I really thought she was just messing with me.

She also said that the fact that she never kept her phone with her while she worked played a big part.

That way she wasn't constantly distracted and allowing her brain to be re-wired by social media.

Those were her words, of course.

She was entering the hallway at the back of the living room on her way to retrieve her phone when I spoke up again.

"Hey, Shay?"

"Yeah?" she turned.

"They're right, you know."

"About what?"

"You do deserve some rest."

"*Pshh*. I don't have time for that. I'll sleep when I'm dead." With that, she quickly turned and disappeared into her bedroom.

Maybe this was better. Things never seem as bad on a full stomach. We would have some dinner and then I could inform her of what a disappointment I am.

3

Sunday, April 18th, 2032

It was 11:50 p.m. That's what the clock said when I looked at it for something like the fifteenth time since I laid down just after 10:00. Having a hard time getting to sleep was nothing new. It was actually a pretty common problem for me, owing to a number of reasons. Such as when Shayra would put on a load of laundry after arriving home late from work. The washer and dryer were just off of the kitchen which also happened to be directly on the other side of the wall from my bedroom. The metal buttons on her jeans would clank against the inside of the dryer drum into the wee hours of the night. Or when our next-door neighbor Mrs. Hartley's dog, a black lab named Daisy, would spend the entire night barking at the trees moving, or some equally ridiculous thing, outside the bedroom window. A bedroom that sadly also shared a wall with mine. This was not Mrs. Hartley's bedroom, mind you, it was Daisy's bedroom. That overprivileged dog had a better life than I did, with its diet of steak and boiled chicken and its pink rhinestone encrusted collar. Not to mention it's privilege to bark as much and as late into the night as it pleased.

But not tonight. Tonight the apartment was silent. Painfully silent. Not even the dull white noise of the air conditioner blowing cool air through the vent on the ceiling. It was that part of the year in central Texas where it was hot enough to need it during the day but at night it would shut off as temperatures dropped down to the high fifties.

No, none of the typical reasons factored in this time. My insomnia on this particular occasion was the result of something different altogether.

Besides being Monday, tomorrow was also Shayra's birthday, and I still hadn't told her that I got fired last Friday. I was left now with only two options, each one somehow feeling worse than the other. Either I ruin her birthday by telling her that, not only did I get fired on Friday, but I lied to her about it all weekend, or

I pretend I still have a job by putting on an elaborate charade, including wearing my Masterson P&P delivery uniform to our traditional birthday lunch.

I was so screwed.

I came to the conclusion that I definitely wasn't going to figure any of this out on an ever increasing lack of sleep and so decided to tackle that problem first. I yanked my blanket back and swung my legs over the side of the bed, every sound exaggeratedly loud in the thick silence of the apartment. As I sat, staring at a random spot on the carpet, the only insomnia remedy I could come up with was a glass of warm milk. I had never tried it and it sounded disgusting, but it seemed to work on all the sitcoms and cartoons. Somewhere, in the back of my mind, I could distinctly remember both Porky Pig and Chandler Bing using it to help them fall asleep.

I pushed myself up to standing and grabbed my phone off of the nightstand. I opened my door as silently as I could and walked out into the hall, passing Shayra's closed door and the open door of the bathroom on my way to the living room. Thanks to the last two hours lying in the dark, my eyes were already well adjusted. I could clearly see the table illuminated by the street light coming in through the dining room window. As I sleepily calculated my trajectory through the poorly lit living room and around into the kitchen where I could finally switch on a light without disturbing anybody, a voice from the darkness jarred me the rest of the way awake.

"Alex," it whispered.

"GOD…" I cried out before forcing composure on myself so that I wouldn't end that sentence in an unsavory way. "…BLESS AMERICA."

I whipped around to see Shayra sitting in her recliner in the dark.

"What in the world are you doing?" I asked sharply.

She stifled a laugh, clearly amused by my fear and sudden patriotism. "Sorry. Couldn't sleep. You?"

"Yeah, uh, I don't think I'll ever sleep again after that."

She allowed herself a chuckle accompanied by the slightest smile. But then her smile faded abnormally quick. She stared thoughtfully into the middle distance. It wasn't unusual to find her up in the middle of the night on her laptop, pouring over her notes with a cup of coffee or catching up on social media since she refused to use it on her phone. But that wasn't the case tonight. Something was off. No computer. No beverage. No blanket over her lap. Something so overshadowed her mind that it precluded any other activity.

"Are you ok?" I asked hesitantly.

"Mm-hmm," she answered without releasing her focus away from whatever distant situation it was that was monopolizing her attention.

"Are you sure?"

"Yep."

It suddenly dawned on me that it was probably after midnight. I raised the phone in my hand for confirmation. 12:01 a.m.

"Hey, it's after midnight! Happy b—"

"Why didn't you tell me you got fired?" she interrupted.

I froze. How did she know about that? Had she known this whole time and was just waiting for me to confess? My initial paralysis only lasted a moment. However, when I opened my mouth to speak, I was unsuccessful.

She stared at me, unwavering, waiting for an answer. Perhaps it was my imagination or guilt, but behind the near detached look of annoyance, I was almost certain I saw hurt.

"Why?" she repeated.

"Shay, I…" I finally managed, before words failed me again.

She stood from her recliner and looked me square in the eyes.

After an uncomfortable amount of time she finally spoke. "I'm making coffee."

We sat at the small table in our dining room. Although I always thought that calling it a dining room was fairly generous. It was more of a foyer leading into the kitchen, with the only real separation from the living room being the line where the carpet changed to wood flooring about two feet behind where I now sat. I stared down at the cup sitting in front of me and absentmindedly ran my finger along the rim.

"I'm sorry Shay. I should've told you," I said, looking up at my sister across the table.

Her left hand gripped the handle of her coffee mug and her right elbow rested on the table next to it, supporting her chin with her right palm. The blue light from the street lamps came in through the dining room window and a warm yellow light came from the vent hood over the stove in the kitchen, bathing her in a glowing contrast of color. Her green eyes stared back at me in the dim light.

"Yeah, you should have. So why didn't you?"

"You know why. It's embarrassing. It's the third time in two years."

"Embarrassing, huh?" she said as she raised her chin up off of her palm and cocked her head to the side sarcastically.

"Yeah, of course it is," I reiterated.

"As embarrassing as this conversation where you are having to tell me anyway and then explain why you lied about it?"

I hesitated. "No, now that you mention it. No, it's not."

"Exactly."

I stared at my coffee again for a moment, guilt keeping me from looking her in the eye.

"How did you find out?" I asked.

"Carl called about ten minutes before you got home on Friday to let me know they needed your uniforms back by Monday."

DANG IT, CARL.

"Why did he call *you*?"

"He said he figured it had a better chance of getting done if he called me."

"Of course he did."

A moment of awkward silence passed before she reached over and softly placed her hand on mine, applying a gentle squeeze of reassurance.

"It's going to be ok, Allie. I make enough money to carry us for a while until you can find something. We'll be fine."

The fact that she called me Allie was a good sign, even though I hated that nickname. It was a telltale indicator that she had switched into compassionate sister mode and usually meant that she had forgiven me. Or that she was at least considering it.

"Speak for yourself," I joked, "the last time I got fired my fiancé left me."

She abruptly pulled her hand back.

"Really, Alex? Is that why you didn't tell me? You thought I was just going to walk out on you like Charlie did?"

Oops.

Charlie was actually Charlotte. But more importantly, she was my ex-fiancé. We dated for about two years before I asked her to marry me. I had just gotten a well-paying job at Lockheed Martin, an aeronautics engineering plant about three miles northwest of Ridgmar. It was the best job I had ever had so the time seemed perfect to start a family. However, when I was fired from that job four months later for failing to follow safety protocols, she broke it off, accusing me of being irresponsible and "not ready for marriage." In hindsight, she probably wasn't exactly wrong.

"No, that's not what I meant," I tried.

I could tell by her skeptical expression and the way her head was cocked to the side that she wasn't buying it.

I hesitated for a moment before being willing to confirm. "Well, maybe I—"

"Oh my gosh!" She threw her head back in frustration.

"Basically everybody else in my life has given up on me, Shayra. Why should you be any different?"

"Because we're family! It doesn't work like that."

"Yeah, I guess. You don't deserve this though."

"Stop it!" She pointed a finger at me. "Stop feeling sorry for yourself. We're not doing that bit."

Her countenance softened again and she lowered her finger as she slowly leaned back in her chair, bringing both hands to rest on either side of her coffee mug.

"I believe in you, Allie," she continued. "I always will. I would go broke betting on you if that's what it came to. Every time."

"Thanks, Shay," I said, trying to control the moisture in my eyes.

"So what happened?" she asked, her tone far less confrontational than before.

"Monday."

"Did you tell them about Justin Bieber?"

"Yeah, apparently Carl had some other complaints too."

"Ugh," she angrily turned her head towards the kitchen, "Carl is a douche."

"Yeah," I chuckled, "he is."

We sat in silence for a moment, me staring down at my nearly empty cup and her staring angrily at imaginary Carl in the kitchen.

"Sorry again that I didn't tell you," I said finally.

"Don't worry about it."

"And I'm sorry that thinking about all this kept you up so late."

Her gaze swung quickly back in my direction. She leaned forward in her chair and her eyes dropped to the teal colored coffee mug in her hands.

"Uh, yeah. No, that's not why I was up," she said as her fingers began fidgeting awkwardly with the mug.

"Oh, really? Why were you up?"

"The Project," she said uncomfortably without looking up.

"Oh, what about it?" I smiled a little. "You know, if you can tell me."

When she finally looked up at me, my smile instantly disappeared. Fear was not a common emotion to see in my sister's eyes, so I almost didn't recognize it. But it was there now, and it was clearly potent. Her eyes darted back and forth across my face. Below the fear I saw traces of indecision. I guessed that she was contemplating how much she could get away with telling me.

She leaned forward and lowered her voice to a whisper. "They're breeding nano-organisms."

"What?"

"They're like microorganisms, but smaller—"

"Yes, I guessed that part. Who is breeding them?"

"Lykos. *Engineering them* would probably be a better term. I don't know how they're doing it. They won't tell us. But they are."

"Why?"

She brushed a strand of red hair out of her eyes. The shadow of the trees outside danced across the left side of her face.

"The guiding force behind Project Nil is the statement 'No disease is incurable'."

"Wait, that's really what the project is called?"

"Alex!"

"Right. Sorry. Go on."

"Anyway, their theory is that these nano-organisms will feed on sicknesses. Bacteria, viruses, even cancer cells. They want to inject them into humans as a way to cure these diseases."

"That sounds—"

"Dangerous? Exactly. It's extremely dangerous. The behavior of these things is frighteningly unpredictable. There is no way to just tell them what to eat. We are decades away from that kind of bio-programming technology. I mean, we're talking about genetic indoctrination, editing instincts on the cellular level." She seemed to notice my eyebrows furrowing, as they tended to when she went too far into scientific jargon, and so she switched gears. "Thankfully right now they only have us running simulations with blood samples from a donor, but they want to start testing on live subjects by the end of next month."

"Have you talked to them about all this?"

"Of course. But they don't want to hear it. They have no interest in actually helping people. They say it's all about advancing knowledge, but when I remind them about the importance of safety, then they go to great lengths to remind me about the weight of stock prices and 'fiduciary responsibilities'."

"That sounds about right."

She leaned back in her chair and shifted her gaze to the ceiling behind me, the relief of finally talking to someone about this clearly giving way to exhaustion. She sat silent for a brief moment before her eyes returned to me.

"I don't want to be a part of this, Allie," she said softly. "They're messing with things they can't possibly hope to control."

"Maybe you could quit. Just tell them all of this and walk away."

"Well I can't now!" she said as she threw her hands up in frustration.

"Yeah," I said quietly, letting my head drop toward the table.

Instantly she realized what she had said.

She closed her eyes and shook her head. "I'm so sorry. That's not what I meant."

"You're not wrong though."

She sat quietly, clearly choosing her next words with great care.

"Look," she started cautiously, "don't worry about it. I'll be fine. *We'll* be fine. I have a busy day tomorrow including our legendary birthday lunch and nothing will be of more help with these problems than some sleep. After all, 'Tomorrow is a new day, with no mistakes in it'."

"*Anne of Green Gables*? Really?"

"Learn to love it," she said snottily as she stood and started towards her bedroom.

"Hey, Shay?" I called after her as she rounded the corner into the living room.

"Yeah?" she turned.

"Happy Birthday."

"Thanks," She smiled warmly and then turned back, disappearing into the darkness of the hallway.

I had heard that quote dozens of times over the last ten years. Even though I didn't love its source, I couldn't deny the truth of it. I stood and made my way towards my bed, not yet fully understanding the gravitas of that statement. It was true, at least for now, tomorrow had no mistakes in it.

4

Monday, April 19th, 2032

Western Place sat on it's own little section of frontage road on I-30, so the most efficient way to get there from Renaissance Gardens was to take a winding back way through the neighborhood. I turned off of Pershing Ave. into the rear entrance of the east parking garage about 11:50 a.m. I climbed out of the car and made my way through the garage and then down a corridor of concrete towards the basement level elevator just inside the building. I pressed the up button and waited a moment before it dinged and rumbled open.

Shayra's lab was on the top floor. Actually, all of the labs at Lykos Biotech were on that floor. She once told me that it was the only way they could install proper ventilation. The ninth floor directly below also belonged to Lykos, but it was mostly offices, a break room and a reception area for visitors. I didn't really feel like I needed to be received, but security procedures required any visitor to the lab to stop at the reception desk. Even those, such as myself, who had undergone the rigorous security screening and background check that they required of recurring visitors. Also, the elevator could only reach the tenth floor when the receptionist gave it authorization from her computer. Said receptionist, a pretty hispanic girl named Shelly, had a bit of a thing for me. She had started at Lykos about four years ago and she had picked up on our birthday lunch tradition the following April. It was the only time she knew to expect me at the office and she tended to dress accordingly. This continued even after Charlie and I started dating. In fact, once Charlie started accompanying us for our yearly lunch, Shelly's tops got progressively lower cut. Charlie was not really the jealous type, but suffice it to say that she and Shelly had a turbulent relationship.

As the elevator opened to the expansive wood trimmed reception area, I could see that today was no exception to her clothing-based attempts to make an impression on me. The reception desk sat about fifteen feet from the elevator door directly ahead of me. On the wall above the desk was a six foot tall brushed aluminum rendition of the Lykos Biotech logo. It was a representation of a molecule or atom of some kind with orbs swirling around it, including one that partially passed in front of the company name that sat prominently in the center.

Shelly spotted me the instant the elevator door opened.

"Hey Lex!" she said as she instinctively tilted her head down and pushed her shoulders forward in an attempt to accentuate her…features.

"Hey…Shelly," I said hesitantly.

Shelly was a sweet girl and classically attractive, but she was also not the sharpest girl to be found. Maybe it was because I grew up around a sister who was brilliant at everything she ever tried, but a girl like Shelly just didn't do anything for me. I kept my eyes fixed on her face, partially to be a gentleman, but also to keep her from getting the wrong idea about my feelings toward her.

"You know Lex is a girl's name, right?" I said with an awkward chuckle.

Her eyes looked off to her right, looking just past me at the ceiling. She absentmindedly chewed her gum as I could almost hear the central control center in her brain waiting for a return signal.

Her eyes turned back toward me. "Lex Luther," she said finally. "He's a man. And a total hottie."

"Yeah. I mean, he's a bad guy."

"Who is?" she said with a blank stare.

I wanted to hang my head in frustration, but that would have left my gaze resting right at the neckline of her red blouse. A neckline that could only be described as "plunging." Instead I turned my head to the left and caught a glimpse of a small red rectangle in the bottom corner of her second computer monitor. It read "*Auth. Elevator.*"

"Hey," I pointed a finger over at the monitor, "that little red button looks like it does something!"

"Yeah," she giggled flirtatiously.

We stared at each other for about ten seconds as I waited for her brain to finish computing what I was trying to imply.

"Is there something else you want me to call you instead?" she asked.

I could practically see the words "system error" flashing across her eyes.

"Just Alex is fine," I sighed.

She smiled through her noisy gum chewing and slowly swayed her shoulders back and forth, trying to draw my attention downward to the outfit she had worn just for me. I couldn't take it anymore.

"Alright. Will I get in trouble if i just…" I reached across the desk towards her computer mouse.

She clearly misinterpreted where I was reaching.

"Not with me," she said in a sultry voice as she raised her eyebrows slightly.

Instantly my hand flew back and found a hiding place, resting on the back of my neck.

"Nope," I said sharply, "can you just…can you authorize the elevator. For me. Please. Shelly. Thank you."

"Sure thing…Just Alex." She smiled.

"Thank you. Thanks. Ok, bye."

I turned back as the elevator doors slid open, still rubbing awkwardly at the back of my neck. Once inside, I turned back to see her still smiling at me. I did my best to maintain a convincingly comfortable expression while subtly reaching down and pumping the door close button. As far as I was concerned, they couldn't close fast enough.

The elevator opened noisily, revealing the nondescript white halls of the tenth floor. This area of the building always felt sterile and bland, so much so that it teetered on the threshold of being unsettling. A flickering fluorescent light down the hall added to the suspense thriller movie motif.

As you would expect at a scientific facility, the layout of the floor plan was fairly logical. Directly outside the elevator door on the left wall was a plain light gray door with a plastic name plate next to it that read "*Lab A.*" Across the hall a little farther down was another door with a plate that read "*Lab B.*" Still further down on the same wall as the first door was "*Lab C.*" This pattern continued all the way down the hallway, turning three corners and ending up full circle with the last lab two doors down from the elevator in the opposite direction from where it started with Lab A. Sixteen labs in all, assigned letters A through P. I always thought it was a little confusing that none of the doors were labeled beyond the assigned letter of the room, but after last night's conversation with Shayra, I was beginning to think the anonymous nature of the outside of the doors was probably intentional.

The last door that completed the circle, just to the right of the elevator, was the only one that had a name on it.

"*Dr. Joseph Gainsborough,*" a black name plate stated blandly.

I knew him as Lykos Biotech's chief scientist and my sister's boss. He and I had only interacted a handful of times, but the exchanges always left me feeling like I had done something wrong, without really knowing exactly what it was.

I glanced at the crack below his closed door and saw that the room was dark. He didn't seem to care for visitors to the tenth floor, so his absence came as a relief. I made my way down the hall and around the corner to Lab H where Shayra worked. As usual, the distinct sound of animal chatter came from behind the door of Lab D. I'd seen it with the door open enough times to know that it was where they kept the animal test subjects. A few chimpanzees in large cages lining one wall and several glass enclosures of various sizes on the other walls containing mice, guinea pigs and rabbits. I reached the door at Lab H and I gave it a gentle knock.

"Come in," came the muffled voice from inside.

I twisted the L shaped handle and swung the door open. Shayra looked up from her work.

"Hey there 'Lex'," she said cheerily.

"Oh my gosh." I rolled my eyes. "Did you see what she was wearing?"

"Every bit of it. She asked me if I thought you would like it."

"What? What did you say?"

She smiled mischievously, "I said absolutely you would."

I gave her my most disappointed frown. She ignored it and chuckled to herself.

"I just have to change and we can go," she said as she turned toward her office at the back of the room.

She walked in and closed the door.

"Have you found any good job possibilities yet?" she continued from the other side of the door.

"Uh, no not really. There's some openings at Lockheed Martin but I'm guessing that's probably not an option. In fact, they probably have a file in HR with my picture in it and the words 'Don't even think about it' stamped across it."

As I spoke, I looked to my right towards the counter where Shayra had been working. On the far end, closest to her office, sat three round plastic dishes, all containing a small amount of thick, red liquid. Human blood, I guessed. Closer to the middle of the counter was an elaborate setup for some sort of experiment she had been preparing. There was a thin metal cylinder with a circular base about four inches in diameter that I recognized immediately as a Bunsen

Burner. A black hose ran from the back side of the base over to a valve on the back end of the counter. A shiny silver handle labeled "*Gas*" was turned perpendicular to the output spout, indicating the gas flow was off. Just behind the base of the Bunsen Burner another circular base held a metal pole in place that stood about two feet in the air. Extending out above the burner was a metal ring attached to the pole a few inches away by screw clamp. Suspended above where the flame would be was what appeared to me as a small, handleless teacup. A triangle made up of small clay cylinders kept the teacup in place while twisted wire arms reached out from the clay to rest on the edges of the metal ring, supporting the triangle. I leaned slowly over the edge of the teacup to confirm my suspicion about its contents. Yep, more blood.

"Maybe I should work here," I joked.

"Uh, yeah, let's put a pin in that," came the response from the other side of the door.

How hard could it really be? I've seen Shayra do this stuff dozens of times.

I picked up the spark lighter sitting a few inches away from the teacup set-up. Remembering some indistinct past instruction I had received from my sister but probably never asked for, I reached over and placed my hand on the gas valve, knowing that you should open the valve and ignite the flame with the spark lighter in quick succession. I turned the handle until it was parallel with the output valve and squeezed the handles of the spark lighter just above the spout as soon as I heard the gas begin to hiss. A small blue flame burst to life at the end of the burner just an inch or so below the white teacup.

"I noticed Dr. Doom isn't here," I said as I watched the flame strain to reach the container resting in the metal ring.

"Yeah, he's at our Oklahoma City lab this week. But you're still not supposed to know anything about this project so don't read anything you see laying around and definitely don't touch-"

The latch clicked and the door swung open. She stopped mid-sentence and her eyes grew wide as she saw my experiment.

"Alex! What are you doing?" she yelled as she lunged across the room, grabbing the gas valve and twisting it aggressively to the off position.

"I was just seeing what happened when I heated up this teacup," I said, reaching towards it.

"It's called a crucible," she snapped as she swatted my hand away, "and don't touch it!"

"Sorry," I apologized as I watched her grab a stack of lids and start covering the plastic trays one by one.

Even still, curiosity dictated that I sneak a peak at the contents of the crucible after my heating experiment. I strained my neck over the top of the metal ring to see inside the opening of the small clay container. As the thick red liquid came into view, I perceived motion inside. The slightest hint of miniature swirls moving in slow motion. Before I could confirm that it wasn't merely a trick of the fluorescent light on my eyes and chemical fumes messing with my equilibrium, Shayra reached in front of me and placed a small round lid over the top of the crucible.

"Come on," she said, grabbing my arm and pulling me towards the door, "before you ruin any more of my samples."

We made our way down the hall to the continued sounds of the animal chatter from Lab D.

"I forgot to tell you," she continued as we arrived at the elevator and she reached to press the down button, "I have to stay at the lab tonight to monitor the samples. That means you'll be on your own for dinner."

"Ah, well…" I started.

"I know, you don't have a job right now." She reached back and pulled her phone out of the back pocket of the jeans she was now wearing. "Here, you can borrow my credit card."

She opened an app on her phone and begin tapping various spots on the screen. I leaned over and read off some of the options she had selected:

Send to: Alex
Credit Line: Full
Expires: Indefinite

"Indefinite?" I asked, surprised.

"Yeah, uh, look, this card has a pretty high limit. Use it when you need it until you start getting a paycheck again."

"Are you sure?"

"Just take it and shut up," she said impatiently as she tapped send.

My phone buzzed in my pocket. I pulled it out and tapped accept on the notification informing me that I had received a loaned credit card.

"Thanks, Shay," I said playfully as I reached over and wrapped my arm around her shoulder.

She instantly started squirming to get out from under my arm. There were few things she hated more than physical displays of affection.

"Stop it or I'm taking it back!"

"Wait," I pulled my arm back as a sudden realization hit me, "what about your birthday evening tradition?"

In honor of her middle name, we had started the tradition a couple of years ago of watching the movie *Titanic* on the evening of her birthday. Both of them, actually. We would start with the original from the year before she was born and then moved on to the remake from a few years ago. We spent most of the latter making fun of the terrible chemistry between Tom Holland and Ariel Winters who play the leads. Although the ending is better since Rose makes room for Jack on the floating plank and they both survive.

"Sorry, I'll have to take a raincheck on that one. Maybe this weekend?"

"Yeah, ok," I said as the elevator let out a ding and the doors slid open. "Come on, lunch is on me!"

I held up my phone that contained her credit card and waved it in the air as I walked forward into the elevator. She threw her head back and sighed as she reluctantly followed me.

5

Tuesday, April 20th, 2032

The ever changing colors from the television flashed across the walls of the otherwise dark living room. I sat alone in my apartment with a half eaten fish taco sitting on its paper wrapper in my lap. Shayra's two least favorite types of food were seafood and Mexican food, leaving fish tacos as the logical choice for an evening when she was working late. I had gotten distracted by my movie and was trying to hurry and finish my dinner before she arrived home.

As I hurriedly scarfed down the last bite of my taco, I felt a vibration coming from beside me on the couch. Shayra's name and contact photo lit up my phone screen.

"Hey," I said as I answered, "you'll never believe this, but the new *Titanic* movie is on TV!"

"Alex," came her voice from the other side.

"Yeah, it just got to the part where Rose says she'll never let go and then doesn't."

"Alex…"

I looked over at the clock and saw that it was five minutes until 8:00 p.m.

"Are you about to head home?" I asked.

"Not exactly."

It suddenly struck me how weak her voice sounded, as if she hadn't slept in days. I reached over and set my empty taco wrapper on the coffee table, as if that would help me to deal with whatever situation was about to present itself.

"What's going on?" I asked, trying not to sound as concerned as I had suddenly become. "Where are you?"

She hesitated for a moment.

"JPS Hospital," she said weakly.

I watched the numbers counting up slowly as I rode the elevator at John Peter Smith Hospital to the fourth floor. Elevator rides always felt slow to me, but with my sister lying in a hospital bed on the other end of this particular ride and almost no details about how she got there, it had reached the point of being agonizing. The doors finally opened and I made my way briskly to the nurses station.

"Shayra Lee," I said while I was still a few feet away.

The nurse looked up from her computer screen.

"Are you family?" she asked robotically.

"I'm her brother."

"412."

She answered quickly without consulting her screen. Something about Shayra's case stood out to her among the dozens of patients she had seen that day if she was able to spout off her room number so quickly from memory. I was in a hurry so I was grateful for the brevity of the conversation and didn't take the time to question it.

The door to room 412 was already open so I peeked my head in to make sure my entering of the room at that moment was allowed. As I rounded the corner of the doorway I saw Shayra lying in the hospital bed. The headrest of the bed was slightly inclined and her usual pony tail had been taken down, leaving a noticeable crease in the red hair that cascaded down the pillow on either side of where her head rested. A nurse with ombre hair that was pulled up into a messy bun stood on the far side of the bed, checking the contents of an IV bag.

"What happened?" I asked as soon as I stepped through the door.

"Uh, I'm not exactly sure." Shayra gave her head a groggy shake as if she was trying to dislodge a jammed memory. "I was standing next to the counter in the lab writing in my notes, then I just started feeling lightheaded. I grabbed the counter to keep from falling but it didn't help. Then I just woke up on the floor."

The nurse came around to the side of the bed where I stood and I extended my hand towards her.

"I'm Alex. I'm her brother."

"Kristen," she said as she accepted my handshake. "I'm your sister's charge nurse."

I glanced down at the name badge that hung at the end of a retractable alligator clip on her scrubs and noticed a pink ribbon sticker affixed to the far left side, across from her picture. A cancer survivor, I guessed.

"Ok so tell me the truth, because I know my sister won't," I said to Nurse Kristen. "How is she really doing?"

"She's fine," she said with a chuckle. "We're just waiting on the results of a few tests so we can know how to proceed."

As she spoke, I noticed Shayra's face beyond her shoulder. It bore a look I had seen many times. She was analyzing. Watching every detail of my interaction with Nurse Kristen. Her eyes were tired, but alert.

"Thanks, Kristen," I said.

She smiled politely and then made her way out the door and down the hall. I retrieved a chair that was positioned nearby against the wall and scooted it over to Shayra's bedside.

"How do you feel?" I asked

"I just feel really weak," she said quickly, her eyes darting back and forth across my face, still analyzing. "How do you feel?"

"Me? I feel fine."

"No symptoms?"

"Symptoms of what?"

"Lightheadedness? Weakness?"

"Do you think this is contagious?"

Her eyes shot to the door and then back. She raised her head up off of the pillow to meet my eye line as much as she could. She lowered her voice and her face got unsettlingly serious.

"Everybody from Lykos is here," she whispered.

"What? Like, here to visit you?"

"No, admitted. With the same symptoms as me. And not just Lykos, everybody in our building. They haven't made that connection yet, or we'd probably all be in quarantine."

"What? What do you think it is?"

"I'm working on it," she said, her eyes still scanning my face. "So, no symptoms?"

"No, nothing. Should I be worried?"

She stared intently for a moment before her face relaxed and she let out an exhausted sigh. She let her head fall back into the pillow.

"No," she said airily, "there's no need for you to worry."

She looked in the opposite direction and weakly reached her arm towards her laptop bag, "Can you hand me my computer?"

I got up from my chair, walked over to her bag and removed the computer.

"Is there anything else you need?" I asked as I handed it to her.

She opened it as quickly as her weak hands would allow and she began logging in.

"I think I just need some rest," she said, her eyes already fixed on the computer screen.

I wanted to point out the fact that typing furiously on a computer was not rest, but at that point she had mostly stopped listening. She was in full analysis mode and nothing short of whatever findings she was looking for would snap her out of it.

"How about I bring you lunch tomorrow? Maybe some Pho?"

She stopped just long enough to smile at me, "That sounds great, Allie. Thanks."

After making her promise to get some actual rest, we said our goodbyes and I stepped out the door. Before I turned to the left I glanced in the opposite direction to make sure my path was clear. My eyes settled on a small waiting area about fifteen feet away and a man who sat there wearing khaki dress slacks and a green plaid shirt. I froze when my gaze landed on his face. He was already watching me.

My eyes instinctively bounced downward to avoid eye contact, landing on the white corner of a name badge that had been haphazardly tucked into his shirt pocket. I could barely see a portion of the logo on it, but I recognized it instantly: Lykos.

Maybe he was one of her coworkers, here to visit her and just waiting until I was done in the room? No, Shayra said everyone from her lab had been admitted to the hospital.

He must have noticed that I spotted the badge because he nonchalantly reached up and tucked it the rest of the way into his shirt pocket.

I turned back the other direction as casually as I could and started toward the elevator. I reached it and pressed the down button, causing the doors to slide open immediately with a ding. As I walked in and turned back to the hallway, I peered down toward the waiting area, trying to catch one more glimpse of the mysterious figure. He remained in his seat, watching me, making no advances towards the door to room 412. He wasn't here to visit her and he certainly didn't look sick. As the elevator door slid shut, the disturbing reality solidified in my mind.

Shayra's room was being watched.

6

Wednesday, April 21st, 2032

Most of the next morning was spent cleaning the apartment. Normally, Shayra did most of the cleaning and I knew whenever she got out of the hospital, the last thing she would want to do was tidy up after the bachelor life I'd been living for the last few days. After a quick trip to Little Saigon to pick up lunch, I arrived at the hospital about 1:00 p.m. As I made my way down the hallway of the fourth floor, I saw nurse Kristen coming out of room 412 with a poorly concealed look of concern covering her face. We met at the nurses station.

"Hey, how's she doing?" I asked.

"Um," she hesitated, "she's…I don't…I don't know. We're running some more tests."

Her head dropped and she suddenly reached up and gripped the edge of the nurses station.

"Are you ok?" I asked as I reached out my hand to offer support.

"Uh, yeah. I just…I just don't feel very good."

"Maybe you should go home."

"No, we've already had tons of people call in today. We're really short handed."

"Um, what exactly are your symptoms?" I asked hesitantly.

She wasn't used to being on the receiving end of that question. "I guess dizzy spells like what I just had. I don't know. I just feel really weak all over."

Before she could even finished her sentence, I took off past her and darted through the door of room 412. Shayra lay on her back, staring towards the ceiling.

"Shay, what's happening to everybody?" I asked pointedly.

"Alex!" She turned her head quickly towards me, her eyes wide and a panic permeating her voice. "They took my laptop!"

"What? Who did?"

"Lykos. Their guy took it back to the lab."

I turned and looked just down the hallway where the man had been the day before. He sat two seats over from yesterday's position reading a magazine.

"Yeah," I said, "why is he sitting out—"

"You have to get it, Alex. My computer, you have to."

"Um, yeah, I'll get it. Don't worry."

She closed her eyes and swallowed hard. A single tear rolled down her cheek.

"Hey," I said as I stepped forward and knelt next to the bed, taking her hand in mine, "what's wrong?"

She took a moment to gather her composure, and it seemed she was having to concentrate on her breathing.

"There's something they're not telling us," she said softly. "There's something they're not telling anyone."

I leaned in closer, "What?"

"They found something. In the blood test they ran yesterday. I saw it on the screen. They found an 'unknown bacteria'."

I glanced just past her at the heart monitor on the other side of her bed. The display read 122 BPM.

"Unknown bacteria?" I asked, trying not to let the number concern me.

"They found something they can't explain in my blood. They think it's a bacteria, but it's not."

135 BPM.

"Shay, your heart rate is kind of high. We should probably call the nurse." I turned toward the door and raised my voice. "Hey Kristen—"

A weak but convincing hand came to rest on my cheek and turned my head back toward the bed.

"They're airborne, Alex," she said, her breathing becoming more labored and her voice more desperate. "The nano-organisms have gone airborne. That's what's in my blood. It's what's in everybody's blood. They're multiplying and they can't be stopped."

159 BPM.

A chill ran down my spine at the words she spoke. The fear in her eyes had returned, and this time it was immeasurable. I pushed passed the paralyzing panic that began to seize me after her statement and frantically searched for the nurse call button. As I pressed it, she reached over and gripped my arm with her hand, her normally rosy cheeks now fading to a pale porcelain.

"It's ok, Alex." Her words came between tortured breathes for air. "You can do this."

"Shay…" I felt a lump rising in my throat.

"Get…my laptop…there's still hope…" she gasped.

"I don't even know the password!" it suddenly occurred to me.

188 BPM.

"Alexander…" Her voice trailed off.

She let out a long exhale and I felt her grip on my arm relax.

"Shay?"

0 BPM.

"Shayra!" I heard myself exclaim, desperation in my voice.

The heart monitor let out a solid high pitched tone.

"Code blue!" a voice behind me shouted.

It was Nurse Kristen. She had arrived in the room moments before the heart monitor had flatlined. Within seconds the room was full of people and activity. An anonymous set of hands pulled me up and away from the bedside, guiding me to the chair that now sat against the wall next to the door. My eyes started to fill with tears as I watched a doctor and a team of nurses surround my sisters lifeless body and begin to prep her for the defibrillator.

"Shock three sixty!" the doctor yelled.

"Shocking three sixty," a voice responded.

"Clear!"

Everyone in the room pulled their hands away and leaned back from the bed as the doctor placed the paddles on Shayra's chest. I heard the high pitched squeal of the capacitors charging followed by an electric pop. Her back arched involuntarily and then fell back into the mattress with a soft thud.

"What do we got?" the doctor said impatiently.

"No response."

"Kristen, start compression! Get a bag mask."

The moisture in my eyes was beginning to turn the frenzied movement of the medical team into a blur of indiscernible white and blue movement. I became acutely aware of the sound of my own heartbeat pounding in my ears as I struggled to catch my breath. I closed my eyes to try to push down the panic that was rising up and focused on listening to the activity in the room.

The high pitched drone of the heart monitor. The hiss of the bag mask. The heavy breathing and grunting of the hospital staff trying to restart my sister's heart.

"No response," Kristen said.

The doctor swore. "Shock again! Clear!"

Another squeal from the capacitors and the electric pop of the defibrillator briefly overtook the sound of the heart monitor.

"Tell me something, Kristen!"

"Nothing!"

Several voices let out various expletives under their breath.

"Again!" the doctor called out to the room. "Clear!"

Squeal. Pop. Thud.

"Clear!" he yelled once more.

Squeal. Pop. Thud.

The frenzy of sounds suddenly fell quiet. I opened my eyes and unsuccessfully tried to blink away the moisture that still clouded my vision. The blurry shapes now stood motionless around the room as I heard a collective sigh from the team. The monotonous drone of the heart monitor was deafening in the otherwise silent hospital room. I held my breath as I listened for the words that I was desperate not to hear.

Finally, the somber voice of the doctor broke the silence, "Time of death, 1:08 p.m."

7

I sat alone in room 412 at JPS Hospital, staring absentmindedly at the bed where my sister had been. The pillow still held the shape of her head and a small damp spot could be seen where her tears had landed only minutes before.

Her last word was my name. Her last word.

That thought should have meant something profound to me but in that moment I couldn't make myself feel it. The numbness had set in as my mind refused to accept what had just happened. A dull, pounding headache was rising up in my temples as I tried, not only to sort through my emotions, but also to make some kind of sense of our conversation. What could possibly be on that laptop that would stop whatever was infecting everybody? And what was I supposed to do about it? Everything I knew about science I had learned from Shayra when she was trying to explain various scientific principles to me. If saving the world had anything to do with the comparative evaporative indexes of rubbing alcohol and motor oil or making a glow stick last longer by sticking it in the freezer, then I was certainly the guy for the job.

Saving the world?

That phrase sounded so ridiculous I almost chuckled out loud. She had said it pretty clearly. They can't be stopped.

But why wasn't I sick yet? And if they really can't be stopped, why had she said there was still hope? None of it made any sense. Even if there was some way to stop all of this, she had definitely chosen the wrong guy.

My eyes fell again on the spot were her head had laid. I felt a fresh pain in my chest and fresh tears filling my eyes as I remembered her words.

"It's ok, Alex. You can do this."

She had believed in me in her last moment and with the last of her strength she had urged me on. Nothing could have summed up our relationship better.

Whatever she had in mind, I had to give it my best shot. I owed her that.

A sharp thud pulled my attention to the hallway. I stood up as quickly as my emotionally drained body would let me and I made my way towards the mounting commotion outside of the room. A huddle of people in blue scrubs surrounded a woman who lay unconscious on the floor. She also wore blue scrubs and through the crowd I could see her ombre hair that—

I let out an involuntary gasp as I recognized her face. It was Nurse Kristen. The heartbreak in my chest began to giveaway to an overwhelming dread.

I had to do something. If only there was someone—

The Lykos guy. Shayra said he had taken her computer. If there were any answers to be had, he would be the one to have them. I turned in a growing rage to confront him, but stopped when it registered on my mind that the room was empty. He was gone.

I turned back around and saw the other nurses helping Kristen up off the floor. She looked confused and weak as they eased her back into a wheel chair. Down the hall, another heart monitor let out a long monotonous tone.

"Code blue! Get a crash cart down here!" a nurse yelled from down the hall.

The code team rushed into the room and the air begin to fill with sounds that were all too familiar.

Squeal. Pop. Thud.

The words of Shayra's warning were becoming reality right in front of me. All the grief and fear I had been feeling begin to fall away, overtaken by one inescapable thought: I had to get that laptop.

I pulled into the rear entrance of the parking garage at Western Place as discreetly as I could manage. If they had a man stationed at the hospital, I had to assume that the lab was being guarded as well. A thought that was confirmed by a car that bore the logo of a privately contracted security company parked in front of the east tower. The garage was empty except for my car and one other. Shayra's Prius sat exactly where she had parked it on Monday after we returned from lunch. I couldn't let myself think about any of that too hard so I put it out of my mind and started down the concrete tunnel that led to the basement entrance.

I pulled Shayra's keys out of my pocket. The basement door was normally left unlocked during business hours, but with all the employees who worked in the building gone, I assumed it would be locked up tight. On her key ring was a small tear drop shaped key fob that would hopefully grant me access to the building. When I reached the door, I touched the fob to the grey rectangle panel and, with a beep, the red light in the top right corner turned green. I pulled the door handle, expecting it to swing open with ease.

No such luck. The door moved about two millimeters before it caught with a metallic clunk. I tried once more with greater force, but the result was the same. I guessed the door had been bolted manually from the inside. I was going to have to try the main entrance and hope I could get past the guard. There was no access to the guest parking lot on the top side from inside the parking garage below so I had to walk out of the garage and down the I-30 frontage road to get up to the main entrance. As I approached I could see the guard standing outside the glass door.

He was a muscular black man who stood at least six feet tall. I guessed by his stance that he was some kind of ex-military. He had both hands behind his back, with the backside of his right hand resting in the palm of his left. I also couldn't help but notice the pistol resting ominously in its holster on the right side of his belt.

"Hey there," I said as I approached, "do you think I could run inside for just a second?"

"Sorry, whole building has been quarantined," he responded, barely looking my way.

"Really, I just need to grab something real quick and I'll be outta here."

"Can't help you."

As I got closer I noticed his forehead was dotted with beads of sweat. That alone wasn't unusual for someone standing outside in that part of the country in April at midday, but he seemed to be struggling to breath and he was clearly having to concentrate on his balance. He swayed just a little and began to lose his balance. Shifting just enough to keep from falling, he quickly settled back into his previous stance.

"Are you ok?" I asked.

"My orders are not to let anyone in the building. Sorry."

I nodded slowly and turned to leave. Before I had made it even ten feet away, I heard a grunt and a succession of thuds behind me. I turned to see the guard lying on the ground, his back up against the glass door of the building. I rushed over to him and nervously felt for some kind of pulse. I had never really tried to find a heartbeat before, so all I could do was to try and duplicate what I had seen in movies. I grabbed his wrist and pressed my thumb just below the palm of his hand.

Nothing.

I tried the other method I had seen in the movies and pressed two fingers into his neck, just below his jaw bone.

There it was. I felt a weak rhythmic beating with my finger tips. As the anxiety of the life or death situation started to pass, I suddenly realized the opportunity that I had been presented with. Without thinking, I grabbed the keys out of my pocket and swiped them across the grey sensor in one motion. The light turned green with a beep and, this time, the door moved easily.

I ran as fast as I could towards the elevator. If the events of the last few days gave me any indication, I had only minutes before the guard woke up. Once inside, I pressed the button for the tenth floor and then pumped the door close button as fast as I could, as if it would actually speed the process along.

When the door finally opened, I found myself staring, not at the blank white walls of the tenth floor, but rather at the reception desk on the ninth floor. But unlike Monday, today the desk was empty.

Everyone from Lykos is here.

"Shelly," I said to myself.

There was no time to think about that right now. I had to get to the tenth floor. Thankfully, I was fairly confident I could handle the situation. I had seen the location of the elevator authorization button on my last visit. Once I made it to the computer, I shook the mouse to get it to wake up. A blue box popped up in the middle of the screen with the Lykos logo just above a text entry field that demanded a password.

Crap.

Anything I could try would be a complete guess, so I would have to make it a good one. I remembered Shayra telling me that they got to choose their own passwords, so long as they disclosed it to the IT department. What did I know about Shelly? She loved to wear low-cut shirts.

"Cleavage," I typed into the text box.

"Incorrect Password," it shot back.

I shook my head, feeling idiotic for actually trying that. What else? Last time I was here she referenced a Superman villain.

"Superman," I typed.

"Incorrect Password"

I wasn't sure how many attempts I had left before it locked me out, so the next one had to count. I closed my eyes and began to sort through every piece of knowledge I could come up with about her.

Come on Alex, think! What is she into? What does she like?

Suddenly it hit me. I felt almost as stupid as when I thought she would make “cleavage” her password.

Me. She liked me.

“Alexander,” I typed.

The password box disappeared and the screen lit up as the computer unlocked.

“Oh, Shelly,” I whispered.

Charlie would have just loved that.

I moved the cursor to her second monitor and gave the red authorization button a click. I had already begun walking toward the elevator when it let out a ding and the doors slid open. Seconds later, it carried me to the tenth floor and I stepped out, making my way briskly toward Lab H to retrieve Shayra’s computer. I had only walked about eight feet when I froze.

Something wasn’t right. I had visited that lab a hundred times over the last ten years but this time something was different. What was it? I looked around as I tried to get a grasp of whatever detail had unsettled me.

My eyes landed on the door of Lab D. The animal chatter. It was gone. I moved closer to the door, listening intently for the whimpers of the chimpanzees and the squeaking mice. Nothing.

Lab D was completely silent.

8

The door to Lab D was unlocked. Because of the security measures downstairs, I guessed they didn't feel the need to secure anything upstairs. It was also safe to assume that once they figured out that some kind of sickness was spreading to everyone in the building, they left in a pretty big hurry and didn't bother to come back and lock up. I opened the door slowly, unsure of what to expect inside. The room was dark with no windows, but the light from the hallway outlined the shapes I remembered from the last time I saw inside the lab. A few large cages lining one wall and several glass enclosures on one of the other walls.

However, this time all the cages were unoccupied. I reached over and flipped the switch just inside the door to the on position. In an instant, what had seemed at first to be simply an empty lab became something much more chilling.

Along the west wall sat eight cages stacked in two rows of four where the chimpanzees had been kept. Three of the cages had bars on the front that had been bowed and bent. I stepped closer reluctantly, almost afraid to know more about what had happened in this room. The three cages with the bent bars also bore scratches all over the front section of bars, as well as smaller, deeper gashes. Teeth marks, I guessed. I looked to the opposite wall where the three glass enclosures sat. The one closest to the back wall was empty, but the other two resembled something from some kind of horror movie. Blood splatters covered about thirty percent of the surface area of the glass. If my memory served me, the one in the middle had contained guinea pigs. I could see the remains of a large plastic exercise wheel in the enclosure had been almost completely torn apart. Among the wood shavings that covered the bottom were shreds of plastic and, on closer examination, bloody bits of white, brown and black fur.

As a nausea began to swell from my stomach and up into my throat, I instinctively turned away from the grizzly scene. My hands came to rest on the island counter that occupied the middle of the room. I lowered my head to let the nausea subside and leaned heavily on the edge of the countertop. After a minute or two, the sickness in my stomach began to fade and I finally felt confident enough to open my eyes again. When I did, I saw a black spiral bound notebook sitting on the counter about two feet to my right. I reached over and slid it across the counter towards me. If all the scientists at Lykos kept notes as detailed as Shayra did, there would most likely be some kind of answers contained within. I came to the last two pages of entries and began reading:

4-19-32, 2:35 p.m.
Cayson Butler
Returned from lunch to find all subjects displaying extremely restless behavior. The chimpanzees are pacing back and forth and aggressively shaking cage doors. The guinea pigs and mice are running in circles and pausing every few seconds to claw frantically at the enclosure glass. Will continue to monitor their behavior closely.

4-19-32, 4:47 p.m.
Cayson Butler
Aggression in subjects has continued to build. Chimpanzees have began biting and pulling at cage doors. Rodent subjects are now using their teeth to destroy their exercise wheel. No cause for this behavioral change has been discovered as of yet.

4-19-32, 5:51 p.m.
Cayson Butler
Aggressive behavior has reached unsafe levels. Chimpanzees are bending cage bars, showing uncharacteristically high strength consistent with elevated adrenaline levels. Will consult with Dr. Gainsborough immediately.

4-19-32, 6:01 p.m.
Cayson Butler
One of the guinea pigs attacked several of the other subjects. Within minutes he had killed the three others with extreme aggression and hostility. I have never observed such violent behavior in rodents.

4-19-32, 6:15 p.m.

Cayson Butler

Mice have began attacking each other with similar hostility as the aforementioned guinea pig. Currently thirteen out of twenty subjects have been destroyed and attacks are continuing even now. Chimpanzees have started injuring themselves by ramming their heads into the cage doors to try and escape. Dr. Gainsburough has authorized euthanasia of all remaining subjects.

I dropped the notebook on the countertop and surveyed the traces of carnage that littered the lab, knowing now what had transpired.

What could have happened to make all these animals lose their minds at the same time? I looked again at the date of the last entry.

4-19-32.

That was Shayra's Birthday. The day I visited the lab. The day before she went to the hospital. There had to be some kind of connection. But if so, why hadn't the animals just shown the same symptoms as her? Every bit of new information just led to more questions. Questions that I didn't have the time to try and answer.

I backed away from the black counter top and turned to walk towards the door. As I reached up to switch off the light, I took one more look at the blood splashed walls of the glass enclosures. Whatever had happened in that room, I wanted no part of it.

The door to Shayra's lab was unlocked. Unfortunately, that was just about the only bit of good fortune that I encountered. I had already searched her office and found nothing so I had moved on to search the lab. My sister always kept things immaculately clean, so I could easily see that the computer was not laying out on the counter. This led me to the conclusion that it would have to be inside one of the many cabinets. I didn't think there was any reason to be subtle about it, so I opened the cabinets one by one and rifled through the contents of each quickly and with no intention of cleaning up after myself. I left a trail of aprons, gloves, petri dishes and various other lab supplies of which I did not know the name scattered haphazardly in my wake. When I reached the final cabinet, my search was abruptly brought to a halt.
It was locked.

I looked around the room for something that could help me access the cabinet that I had started to believe was the most likely in the room to contained the item in question. Beyond the disarray I had left around the lab, I noticed a familiar item. The metal pole with the heavy circular base that had held the crucible above the Bunsen burner sat tucked away in the southwest corner of the room. I grabbed the pole with both hands and carried over to the cabinet. I raised it above my head like a golf club and let the weight carry it down in a destructive pendulum motion. The blow landed diagonally just below where the keyhole was located, separating that part of the particle board door from the rest with a loud sonance of wood and metal. The recoil from the hit caused the cabinet door to swing open and the severed corner to fall to the floor. Triumphantly, I knelt down to retrieve my prize of…

Notebooks. Stacks and stacks of black spiral bound notebooks.

The laptop wasn't here.

9

For the next couple of hours, I sat on the lab floor pouring through Shayra's notes. If I couldn't find her computer, maybe her notes could give me some kind of clue about what she wanted me to do. I estimated there were about sixty notebooks, dating all the way back to June of 2024. That was when she finished her internship and became a full fledged research associate. I could still remember when she came home talking about her first project. Something about PCR and genome randomization. I didn't understand most of what she said of course, but I remember the way her whole face would light up when she would talk about yeast extraction and DNA melting. I specifically remembered that last term because I thought it also sounded made up, just like flavonoids. As I looked at the stacks of notebooks, stained in various spots with chemical spills and splatters, I desperately wished I had time to sit and read them all. To hear new words in my sister's voice one more time, if only inside my head, was all I wanted in that moment. But it was a nostalgia that time wouldn't afford me.

That would have to wait. I was working on borrowed time and couldn't allow myself to get caught up in sentiment.

I reached for the last stack of notebooks that I had pulled out of the cabinet. If there was any logic to their order (and if I knew my sister, there was) then this stack should contain her most recent entries. She always used the first page as a sort of title page where she would write the project name, her name, and the dates that the entries spanned. I picked it up and opened the black cover.

Project Nil
Shayra Lee - Lead Project Manager
3.25.2032 -

Shayra's handwriting. I could hear the words in her voice. A lump rose up in my throat and I covered my mouth as if to stop a sob that hadn't formed yet. This was going to be harder than I thought. Less than two hours ago she had been alive. Now her voice in my head was all I had left of her. I had to press on. I had to put it aside. There would be time to fall apart later.

I flipped to the next page and began reading the first few entries in my head, this time in my voice.

3.25.2032, 5:32 p.m.
Shayra Lee
"No disease is incurable."
Project Nil is officially underway. I met with Dr. Gainsborough about the specifics of the project earlier this afternoon. We will be growing synthetic bacteria that will be used in battling currently incurable illnesses such as lymphoma, HIV, and even viral infections. He requested that I secure a blood sample for growing the bacterial cultures. He said 450ml should be sufficient for the time being. Once the sample is secured he estimates the bacteria should reach maturity in approximately one week.

3.26.2032, 3:08 p.m.

Shayra Lee

After further discussion with Dr. Gainsborough, I have found out that what we are creating is in fact not bacteria, but a sort of bacterial-protozoal hybrid. A "nano-organism" with the eukaryotic characteristics of a protozoan but with the ability to self replicate like bacteria through binary or possibly even multiple fission. I advised him that any results of such genetic manipulation would be unpredictable and therefore irresponsible. I was told in no uncertain terms that the project will continue "with or without" my participation.

With or without her participation? Why would she stay and help with the project if she knew it was unsafe?

4.6.2032, 4:00 p.m.

Shayra Lee

I have secured 450ml of blood from a donor as requested. I have passed it on to Dr. Gainsborough to begin the growth process.

Donor name: A. Lee.

I had to stop and read that foot note again.

A. Lee?

April 6th was the day that I had given blood at lunch. Shayra had been insistent that I should go and donate blood. She was relentless for a week and a half before I finally gave in.

"It's your responsibility as a healthy human adult," she had said.

Or rather she had *lied.* Why had she needed *my* blood for this project? Further reading gave me no explanation of what part I played in all of this. The entries picked up on April 14th after, I presumed, the one week growth period mentioned in the first entry.

The next few pages detailed three days of experiments with various chemicals and compounds to try and stimulate some sort of reaction from the newly created organisms with, as far as I could understand, limited to no results. I felt the muscles at the base of my skull begin to tighten as I came to the last entry from the Friday that I got fired.

4.16.2032, 1:31 p.m.

Shayra Lee

All experiments thus far have yielded no change in N.O. behavior. Subjects remain mostly inactive and show no signs of replication. Dr. Gainsborough insisted that I begin a series of experiments based on thermal variations, starting with rapid heating using a Bunsen Burner. I feel that these experiments could yield unpredictable and possibly dangerous results. I have an appointment with Dr. Gainsborough at 2:00 p.m. to discuss it further. I intend to tell him that I feel this move irresponsible and inadvisable. Hopefully he will listen.

But he hadn't. In fact, I would guess that meeting is why she was sent home early that day. I could imagine how that conversation had gone, especially since I had often been on the receiving end of such soliloquies.

"You need to go home and think about your future at this company," was usually the general message.

She had mentioned the new round of experiments when we had talked on Friday. In fact, the following Monday when I had come by to meet her for lunch, I had seen—

Oh my God.

An aggressive nausea began to rise up in my stomach and move into my throat as the possibility assaulted my mind.

Could it have been me who—

I had to know. I forced myself to continue reading.

4.19.2032, 11:40 a.m.
Shayra Lee
I have prepared a 15ml blood sample containing 10000ppm of the N.O.s in a porcelain crucible for the first of the thermal variations experiments. I will heat the sample quickly to 40°C and monitor closely to see if there are any changes.

4.19.2032, 11:50 a.m.
Shayra Lee
Upon further consideration I have decided the experiment should be done in a sealed environment. Doing so with a Bunsen Burner will present a logistical challenge. I will need to do some research.

That didn't make any sense. Shayra was brilliant and figuring out how to heat a sample in sealed conditions would have been a walk in the park for her. The only explanation is that she was trying to put off doing the actual experiment. She was stalling.

4.19.2032, 1:30 p.m.
Shayra Lee
I decided to proceed with the experiment as originally planned. At 12:00 p.m. I heated the sample to approximately 32°C, covered it and left for lunch. Three samples sat opened nearby on the counter and were also covered quickly after heating the first sample. When I returned from lunch all four samples had shifted in color from bright red to a dark, almost purple. Upon examination under a microscope I found all four samples to be completely devoid of red blood cells. The color change is presumably because the loss of the red blood cells would cause the sample to no longer be infused with oxygen. The N.O. count however, has increased exponentially. I estimate two to three hundred times. The same high levels are found in the samples that had been nearby. This indicates that the N.O.s can travel through the air. My conclusion is that exposing the sample to heat activated the replication process. Based on the

time frame it is also clear that the N.O.s became air borne almost immediately after beginning the replication process. This experiment conclusively proves that these N.O.s are a danger to the human population. The average human body temperature is nearly identical to the temperature needed to activate replication in the nano-organisms. Meaning as soon as they find a host, exponential replication will begin instantly and the new nano-organisms will spread through the air, looking for a new host. This process will continue until every human being on the planet becomes infected. I will be suspending further experiments and dedicating my efforts to finding a way to stop them from spreading.

My hand fell limp, causing the notebook to slip from my grip and land on the counter top. The noise created from the metal spiral binding hitting the counter only registered on my brain as a distant echo. I couldn't process anything other than the words I had just read and, more importantly, what it meant.

It was me. I did it.

I had caused the downfall of the human race. But as heavy as that thought was, another weighed on me even more unshakably in that moment.

I killed Shayra.

The nausea that had been rising in my stomach earlier had now become overpowering. I stumbled a few feet to my left and fell to my knee, reaching for the nearby trashcan as the nausea overtook me.

10

I sat again on the floor of Lab H, my head still reeling from the emotionally fueled vomiting I had just experienced. I stared blankly at the white cabinet in front of me trying to put the surreal information I had just discovered into some semblance of context in reality. I was unsuccessful.

How do you convince your brain that you killed everyone? That you are solely responsible for the end of the world?

I tried to lift my hand to wipe the remaining vomit from my chin, but my arm refused.

Where could I possibly go from here? What could I do? But more importantly, what hope could Shayra possibly have been talking about? Without her laptop, I would probably never know.

A second wave of emotional realization rushed over me. I had caused the death of everyone I had ever known. Shayra, my parents, Charlie, My third grade teacher Mrs. Naden, Carl, Shelly, Dr. Gainsborough, the Lykos guy from the hospital—

Their guy took it back to the lab.

A new anxiousness seized me as thoughts suddenly began swirling in my head.

The Lykos guy. Would he have known what lab Shayra used? There were no identifiers on the outside. He wouldn't have brought it here. What would he have done with it? Where would he put it? A new sense of purpose quickened my mind and restored motor function to my body. I stood quickly and this time successfully wiped the remaining vomit from my chin. I knew where the computer was.

Dr. Gainsborough's office was the only door on the tenth floor that was locked. At least the only one out of the three doors I had concerned myself with. It was a thick wood door with light gray paneling on the outside and a nameplate directly in the center, just below eye level. It looked sturdy, but not what I would call impenetrable. I stepped backwards to the other side of the hall and prepared to charge the door. I felt like one hundred and sixty-eight pounds traveling at whatever speed I could get up to after running for eight feet should be plenty enough force to—

A sharp pain shot through my shoulder and into my back as I bounced off of the middle of the door and fell comically to the ground, landing directly on my back. I let out a loud groan, partially in frustration but mostly the result of the pain. I rolled to my front and laboriously raised my body to a standing position as I mentally prepared for another attempt. I turned to study the door that, despite my action-hero-like efforts, was still standing.

Why had I tried to hit it in the middle? Every movie I had ever seen shows the breaker of the door kicking it a few inches above the deadbolt. Unless it's a comedy, in which case they do exactly what I just did and have pretty much the same results.

After what turned out to be too little thought, I decided to try the kicking method. I balanced on my left leg and raised my right leg as high as I could manage. The impact landed just above the deadbolt as planned, but I had failed to consider the shift in balance as my foot hit the door. I began to fall backwards and so I instinctively reached and grabbed the door handle to stabilize myself. However it turned out to be far too late to recover my stance and the inertia of my already falling body coupled with the contact points of my left leg on the ground and both hands on the door handle propelled me in a pendulum motion toward the wall. On impact my head snapped to the right and hit the wall just above my already hurt shoulder. I let go of the handles and tumbled to the ground in a sore heap of failure.

"Why did Shayra think I could do this?" I mumbled to myself.

It didn't matter. I had to try. And I had to keep trying until the moment that I physically couldn't try anymore, which, if I was honest, didn't feel that far away. I placed my hands flat against the ground and pushed against it to help myself stand once more. I winced at the pain, involuntarily shifting the majority of my weight over to my left arm and shoulder. With much effort and groaning, I finally brought myself again to a standing position. The only plan I could come up with was to charge the door again but with better planning and impact placement. I walked slowly to the other side of the hall and turned again towards the door. I lowered my head and took a deep breath.

This is going to hurt like crap.

Before I could talk myself out of it, I sprinted across the hall towards the door. Every sore muscle screamed at me to stop but I wouldn't let myself listen. I made contact a couple of inches to the left of the handle and deadbolt lock. As I did I heard a cracking sound. The searing pain in my shoulder told me it was my bones cracking, but logic told me it was the door losing its integrity. One more good hit and it would surely give way. I stepped back across the hall and charged at the door one more time, again resisting the last minute urge to turn my hurt shoulder away from impact.

It worked. A little too well. As the door of Dr. Gainsborough's office burst open it occurred to me that I had neglected to calculate a trajectory beyond the door and I found myself falling headlong over the two chairs that sat opposite his desk. In my stumbling, I kicked one of the chairs against the wall and landed with my full weight on the other, causing one of the legs to snap off under the pressure of the collision. With a crash, I came to rest on top of what remained of the broken chair, my back contorted into a painful and awkward position and my shoulder throbbing intensely. With a loud groan, I rolled off of the chair onto the floor, using my forearms to stop my face from hitting the ground. I painfully raised my self to standing again, taking a scan of the room as I straightened my back. There, sitting on top of the bureau, was a small metallic rectangle.

"Bingo," I said for the first and hopefully the last time.

Before I let myself get too excited, I had to make sure it was hers. I limped over and opened the screen. As it lit up, her desktop picture appeared for just a moment before a text box demanded her password.

I remembered that picture. I took it the first night we spent in our new apartment at Renaissance Gardens. It was a picture of Shayra and me, obviously taken when she was fighting the idea of being photographed. She hated how she looked in pictures because of her freckles, but the circumstances under which this one had been taken gave it just enough motion blur to soften them. Between that and the huge, playful smiles we both bore it had become her favorite picture of us and the only picture of herself that she actually liked.

I closed the screen quickly, tucked the computer under my arm and limped out the door towards the elevator. I made it about six feet outside the door before a loud roar stopped me in my tracks. I didn't have to listen for very long before it became obvious what it was. The unmistakable roar of jet engines and the repetitive thwack of spinning blades. Helicopters, several of them by the sound of it, close enough that the building was beginning to shake. I ran as fast as I could down the hallway to Lab J, which occupied that corner of the building from where the noise seemed to be emanating. I could feel the shaking beneath my feet getting more intense as I burst through the unlocked lab door just in time to see three army green Blackhawk helicopters fly past the north window. I had seen that logo before. The white square containing a red plus sign. My father had written a story for the Times Record News about that branch of the armed forces when I was thirteen. They were National Guard helicopters. And they were heading towards the western city limits.

As I watched them retreat I felt something unusual: Nothing. The sight of three military helicopters flying purposefully toward the edge of a town, *my* town, as I knew a deathly epidemic was spreading unstoppably made me feel nothing.

Why? Why wasn't I panicking? I should be feeling dread, anxiousness, or at the very least uncertainty. But in that moment the only emotion I felt rising up was terror. Not terror at what I had just seen, but terror at the numbness that was spreading through my mind.

The military is here.

Nothing.

The world is ending.

Still nothing.

My sister is dead.

Nothing.

I stood staring dead eyed out the window, trying to call before my mind any emotion I could think of. Joy, melancholia, fear, empathy, and sadness all came up empty.

Suddenly I felt something. Something rising up from deep. What was it? What was the emotion that finally broke through? I felt my fist tightening as I caught a glimpse of my reflection in the glass.

Anger. That was what I was feeling.

Before I even realized what I was doing, I had picked up a small centrifuge machine off of the nearby counter and hurled it at the window as hard as I could. It bounced off with a crash, sending a piece of the outer casing flying across the room and leaving a crack in the window where it impacted. Without hesitation, I picked it up and threw it again, this time it crashed violently through the window, sending glass flying in every direction. The cool wind rushing through the broken window revealed multiple cuts along my arms that the broken glass had inflicted without my notice. I raised my right arm to examine one particularly nasty laceration. The warm blood running down my arm combined with a distant yet noisy crash from the centrifuge landing on the concrete below jarred me back to reality. As I turned towards the door, I picked the laptop up off of the counter, thankful that I had maintained enough presence of mind to not throw it at the window. The blood on my arm was smearing along the silver body of the closed computer.

I didn't care. Little things like that didn't really mean anything to me now. I had a task to complete, but at this point I wasn't even sure if I believed in that anymore. I walked, emotionless, down the hall and boarded the elevator. The ride to the first floor seemed profoundly fitting of my current state of mind. Slow and quiet with an inevitable and inescapable ending. As it slowed to a stop and the doors rumbled open, an unexpected shape caught my attention. The view of the expansive first floor lobby was obstructed by the shape of the security guard I had encountered outside. He saw me the same time I saw him and he instantly reached for the laptop under my arm.

There it was. The fear was back.

11

My instincts kicked in as the man's hand was about four inches away from Shayra's computer. I actually didn't realize I had instincts until that moment, but my brain began a quick analysis of the situation before I even realized what was happening.

The guard stood a good six inches taller than me. I would guess someone in his position was trained to react to unexpected situations. But there was something else. Something that didn't fit with the spontaneity of the moment. What was it?

His hand. I had the laptop tucked under my right arm and held discreetly at my side, and yet he had begun to reach for it before the elevator door had even finished opening, before his brain could have possibly finished processing what he saw.

Unless he was expecting me to have it.

As I watched him reach for the computer with his left hand, it was actually the movement of his right hand that arrested my attention. It was moving in the opposite direction with military precision toward—

The gun from his belt was already in his grip before I could react. My muscles finally began to work again, reacting to my brains realtime analysis. I swung the computer up and to the left, bringing it to rest against my chest. My left arm came from the other side to secure my grip and prevent a one handed grab, which is all he could manage with a gun in the other hand; A gun that was now almost pointed at my torso.

Before he could get his weapon in place, I lifted my foot and rested it against the back wall of the elevator about twelve inches behind me. He was infected and weak. I had seen him falter just minutes before. I knew this was my only chance to overpower him. I used my foot to propel myself forward, turning to the left and ramming my shoulder —my *hurt* shoulder — into the middle of his chest.

With a harmony of groans we crashed to the hard marble floor, me on top still refusing to release my grip on the computer but consequentially unable to catch myself. As I bounced off of him and went sliding across the slick floor, I heard his weapon also clatter to the ground. If I had any chance of escaping this situation, it was right now. I jumped up as quick as my aching body would allow and began to run towards the stairs that led to the basement level and the parking garage. Every step caused a shooting pain from my shoulder down my entire left side. My mind was racing as I quickly struggled to review the facts of what had just happened.

Not only was he expecting me to have that computer, but he had reached for his weapon almost instantly. The only possible explanation for that chain of events is that he had been told to prevent anyone from taking that laptop, and if necessary, to employ deadly force.

What had my sister gotten involved in? What could be on her computer that could possibly justify the use of—

My thought process was interrupted by a resounding pop from behind me followed almost instantly by a bullet impacting in the wall directly in front of me, leaving a cloud of gray dust from the sheetrock.

For a moment, I was relieved that he had missed, but that relief didn't last long. A searing pain on the outside of my thigh sent me into a hopeless stumble. My steps faltered just as I was rounding the corner beyond his line of sight, clutching the side of my leg in pain as I hit the floor. I landed on my back, this time unable to maintain my hold on the computer. It slid from my grip and came to rest a couple of feet away. Instinctively, I brought the hand that had been clutching my leg up to where I could see it. There was blood, but not as much as I would have expected. I contorted my body on the ground in a way that gave me a clear view of the wound. The bullet had torn a hole in the side of my jeans as it grazed my leg.

I groaned in pain as I forced myself off of the ground, snatched the laptop from the floor and began moving again. Just before I burst through the door into the stairwell that led to the underground parking area, I turned to see if the guard was coming behind me. I expected to see his weapon raised, finger on the trigger, ready to put an end to my escape.

I saw no trace of him behind me, but instead heard the main glass doors of the building open on the other side of the lobby. He must have decided that he would not be able to catch me on foot in his weakened state. He was going for the vehicle I had seen parked in front of the building.

It didn't really matter now, as I was only a matter of feet from my car. I climbed in quickly and struggled to get the key in the ignition. As I turned the key, a familiar whirring sound indicated that the starter mechanism had once again failed to engage.

"Are you kidding me?" I yelled at no one.

I tried again with the same results. I leaned back in defeat and settled into the seat. The adrenaline that was still pumping through my veins kept my heartbeat so elevated that I could practically hear it in the otherwise silent car.

There was nothing else I could do. I was trapped. Alone in an almost empty parking garage. Just my car and one other—

Shayra's Prius.

I still had her keys in my pocket. I jumped out of my car, not even bothering to close the door, and sprinted across the expansive concrete structure, each step counting down the distance to my salvation.

As I reached the door, I heard the squeal of tires behind me. The security guard's vehicle had entered the front entrance of the garage and was speeding towards my position. I climbed in to the Prius as fast as I could, not thinking about the blood I was smearing from my leg to the leather seat. I tossed the computer in the passenger seat as carefully as time would allow before I reached up and mashed the push button start with all of my adrenaline. I hesitated for a moment waiting for the engine to roar to life until I remembered that this particular car didn't engage the engine until it reached five miles per hour. In frustration I slammed the gear selector into reverse, glancing to the left to check the position of the security vehicle. It was close, about fifteen feet, and it wasn't slowing down.

I slammed the accelerator to the floor, causing the car to lurch backwards. I guessed he had been aiming for the driver side door in an attempt incapacitate me with a direct impact. However, he failed to compensate for my sudden movement and the front end of his car connected with the driver side front fender at what I guessed to be about forty miles per hour, sending the front end of Shayra's car sharply to the right.

The two vehicles now sat parallel, both facing to the east. I reached up and pulled the gear selector down two slots into the drive position just in time to see the guard aim his weapon in my direction. I turned the wheel hard to the right as I once again slammed the accelerator to the floor. I heard his tires squeal again as he followed after me.

I sped towards the front entrance with his car inches from my back bumper. About thirty feet outside the garage entrance sat the concrete wall that divided the frontage road from the busy highway. I accelerated as quickly as I dared, easing off just enough to make the turn. I burst into the sunlight and mashed the accelerator once more, this time without holding back. I looked in the rearview mirror just in time to see the security guard's vehicle also emerge from the gray structure. However, unlike me, he showed no signs of turning.

The front end of his car collided hard with the divider, sending debris flying in every direction and lifting the back of his car a foot and a half off of the ground before it bounced back down to rest on the asphalt.

My foot moved to the left and depressed the break pedal, bringing me and the damaged car to a screeching halt. I waited for what felt like an eternity to see if I could spot some movement inside the vehicle.

What happened? Did this highly trained security guard suddenly just forget to turn the steering wheel?

Even as I wondered, a deeper part of me already knew. I had seen it too many times today.

I exited the Prius and walked cautiously to the driver side of the security vehicle. The guard's lifeless body was hunched over, leaning forward on the steering wheel, fresh blood dripping down the side of his face and onto the deflated airbag. A plume of smoke billowed out as I opened the driver side door. I reached in and pressed two fingers against the underside of his neck as I had done before, but this time there was no question. He was dead. And I guessed it was not the crash alone that had killed him.

As I tried to pull my eyes away from his limp body, my phone begin to vibrate, accompanied by a tone that I recognized as an emergency alert. I pulled the phone from my pocket and raised it to a position that would allow me to read the notification in the harsh afternoon sunlight.

> *Attention: The CDC has issued an immediate quarantine for Dallas-Fort Worth and the surrounding areas. Please stay indoors and await further instructions.*

My arm fell involuntarily to my side as I felt the blood begin to drain from my face.

This was it. The end of the world had officially begun.

12

By the time I got home, the numbness had fully set in. I sat, frozen on the couch in my apartment at Renaissance Gardens, staring blankly at the news report on the television. A pretty blonde anchor in a cream colored blouse was detailing the events of the last couple of days. Or the version they wanted the public to know anyway.

"Hospitals in the DFW area are struggling to keep up the crowds of people flooding in," she said as the broadcast cut to footage of an overrun hospital emergency room and then back, "made increasingly more difficult by dozens of hospital employees becoming ill with the same symptoms. Though it is mostly localized in the metroplex area, some cases have been reported as far away as Wichita Falls. Officials are asking that anyone displaying the following symptoms…"

I had been watching for about an hour and they were starting to repeat themselves. I switched my focus from the television to the computer sitting in my lap. I opened the lid and stared at the login screen. The Picture of Shayra and I laughing was a cruel and ironic contrast to the current situation.

How am I even supposed to access this thing?

My sister was far too careful to pick a password I could guess. It was most likely some string of numbers, letters, and symbols she had picked at random. And even if she had written it down, she would never have kept it somewhere that could be easily discovered. She was careful and thorough. It was one of the great things about living with her. She would always check the locks on the doors three or four times every evening and would never forget—

The audio on the TV tore me away from my memories.

What did they just say?

I picked up the DVR remote, rewound ten seconds and pressed play. The audio began mid-sentence.

"—over five hundred confirmed cases of what experts are now calling 'The Shayra Lee Epidemic,' named for the scientist responsible for the disease and who, earlier today, became its first fatality."

In anger I stood quickly to my feet, gripping the remote so tightly I could hear the plastic creaking in protest. A second figure appeared on the screen. I recognized him immediately. Dr. Gainsborough stood behind a podium with about fifteen microphones attached to the top as he read a prewritten statement.

"We at Lykos Biotech are shocked and horrified by Miss Lee's failure to follow safety protocols and her complete disregard for, not only her co-workers, but the entire human race. I want to assure everyone that those of us who remain at Lykos will not rest until we have found a cure for this plague—this crime against humanity—that Miss Lee has perpetrated in the name of science."

I couldn't take it anymore. I reared back and threw the remote at the television as hard as I could, leaving a spider web of cracks at the point of impact and a pattern of random colored bars covering about half of the screen area. I collapsed back onto the couch and covered my face with my still shaking hands, reeling from the statement I had just heard.

They were blaming everything on her.

I ran my thumb mindlessly across the edge of the phone in my hand. I had to call my parents. I had to tell them what happened.

My dad worked at a newspaper, so the chance that he hadn't already heard the official word on all of this was slim to none. Now my task was to call and explain to him that the blame for the end of the world didn't rest on his late daughter, but on his disappointing screw-up of a son.

It would be ok. Even though they never said it, I guessed they had given up on expecting good things from me long ago. Although I would hope their poor expectations of me stopped short of me being the cause of the apocalypse.

I raised the phone and opened my contacts. I scrolled through the A's, then the B's, but stopped short of the entry that read "Dad" when I came across another name in the C's.

I hadn't spoken to Charlie in at least six months, but I could still remember when I created that contact entry almost three years ago.

I met her at a coffee shop not too far away in Arlington Heights called Craftwork Coffee. It was a unique place with a public coffee shop in the front and individual and team workspaces in the back that could be rented monthly if you wanted to smell coffee all day while you work. Which didn't sound half bad to me.

I could be found at Craftwork fairly often since it was the closest coffee shop that wasn't a major corporate chain. The whole store was white with dark wood accents, leaving a distraction free environment for me to work on the life changing projects that I poured my weekends into.

On that particular Saturday, I think I was working on my pitch for a new sitcom idea or some other way of getting rich without having to do any actual work. I had finished said pitch and was heading towards the door when I saw her.

She sat at a table in the corner reading a book. An actual book. As if that wasn't unusual enough, her hair was parted directly in the middle with one side vibrant pink and the other side a sunflower yellow. With her head hung over her book, the last inch of her hair rested on the table top. She must have felt my gaze on her because her head shot up and our eyes met.

She was pretty. But not just the kind of pretty that made a girl hard for a guy like me to talk to. She was the kind of pretty that created an instant urgency to talk to her because seeing a girl this beautiful in real life was a once in a lifetime occurrence. When she smiled politely in my direction, I knew I had to say something.

I think "Woah..." was the opening line I chose.

Lucky for me she found my reaction at least a little cute, causing her to let out an involuntary chuckle.

"Um…sorry," I said awkwardly. "I just mean 'woah' like you have a...you're a..."

Her smile widened in amusement.

"Uh-huh," was all she replied.

"Um, Alex," I finally managed, reaching my hand towards her and, for some reason, turning my face away until my gaze was sidelong.

"Charlotte. What's wrong with your face?"

"Um, I'm trying not to stare at your...at you. I mean I want to, but I just...I mean, I like your hairs. Your hair. The hairs on your head."

"Wow. You suck at this!" she said with a laugh. "That's adorable. You can sit if you want."

And I did. And we talked about everything and nothing for the next three hours. It felt like one of those dreams that make you really mad when you wake up and realize none of it was real. But it was real. Not only had I met the most beautiful girl in the world, but she found my awkwardness completely endearing.

Before she left, I entered her name and number into my phone. I said "Charlotte" out loud as I typed it into the name box. She reached over and rested her hand on mine.

"Charlie," she said. "Call me Charlie."

As she walked out of the coffee shop that day I knew I was the luckiest man on the planet. I felt ten feet tall and spent the rest of the day with in irrevocable smile on my face. I couldn't wait to tell Shayra.

The thought of my sister brought me back to reality. I was once again alone in my apartment with my phone in my hand.

So much had changed. I hadn't smiled like I did that day in a long while. Sure, the world was ending and that played a pretty big part. But if I was honest with myself, I hadn't been really happy since—

Before I realized what I was doing I had tapped on her name. I nearly threw the phone in my panic, but instead somehow found the courage to raise it to my ear. I hadn't the slightest idea what I was going to say if and when she answered.

Four rings and it went to her voicemail.

"Hey, it's Charlie," the recording started. "You can leave a message if you want but let's be real, I'm just going to text you to find out why you called anyway. So good luck!"

That made me chuckle. I hadn't heard that message yet. Charlie was easily bored so she liked to keep things fresh. It's why she changed her hair color every couple of months.

Beep.

"Hey, Charlie," I said somberly. "Look, I know we haven't talked in a while. I just needed to tell you a couple of things."

I paused for a moment to collect my thoughts.

"I'm sure you've heard on the news about the thing here in Fort Worth, and how everybody is getting sick. Well, it's actually quite a bit worse than they are telling people. There's these nano-organisms that are getting into people's blood, and once you're infected, you only have about two days to live. Apparently it travels through the air and it can't really be stopped. I remember you talking about moving out of the city but I'm not sure where you ended up so hopefully you get this message in time. I guess depending on how far away you moved you may already be—"

I couldn't even make myself say the word. I hung my head and closed my eyes, trying to regain my composure and not convey the absolute emotional wreck I was becoming.

"Listen," I continued, "you need to know that no matter what they are saying, this wasn't Shayra's fault. Ok?"

I paused again. What else could I say? For all I knew, she would never even hear this message. And if she did, it wouldn't make much of a difference anyway.

"I just want you to know I'm sorry. For everything. I know I hurt you pretty bad and you didn't deserve it. So I'm just...sorry. I know you asked me not to call. But, um," —my voice began to break— "the world is ending and I just...I thought of you."

I took a deep breath and let it out slowly.

"Ok. That's all. I lo— I...uh...will talk to you later. Maybe. Ok, bye."

I tapped the button to end the call and let the phone fall out of my hand and onto the couch. There was no more holding back the emotions of the day. I buried my face in my hands, and for the first time since my sister died, I wept.

13

Thursday, April 22nd, 2032

I had tried both of my parents phones two different times now with no luck. Exhaustion had finally overtaken me the night before and I had fallen asleep on the couch before I had a chance to call them. It was now 10:00 a.m. and I had been awake for about an hour. I was getting ready to pour myself a bowl of cereal before trying again when my phone started vibrating on the table.

"Hello?" I answered quickly.

"Alex?" came my dad's concerned voice from the the other end.

"Where have you been? I've been trying to call you all morning!" I said more impatiently than I intended.

"We're at the cabin in Ruidoso. We don't get any cell signal up there. I came into town to run to the store and overheard a couple of ladies talking about some kind of situation in the Fort Worth area. What's going on?"

"The whole city is under quarantine. Dallas too. There's an airborne virus that's spreading really fast."

"Dadgum. Well, are y'all ok?"

My heart sank.

"Y'all?"

"Yeah. You and Shay."

"Dad, Shayra is…"

I stopped suddenly. When my parent's vacationed, they vacationed all the way. They stayed in a cabin about forty minutes outside of town, which is why they couldn't get any cell reception. Since he worked at a newspaper, he refused to watch the news or read a newspaper as a way to really disconnect.

"The world will still be there when we get back," he would always say.

Except this time it wouldn't.

At this point, my parents were probably some of the only people left in the country who didn't know what was happening. And I couldn't bring myself to take that from them.

"Shayra and I are just fine," I continued, trying to hold back the lump that was rising up in my throat. "She's working on some kind of solution for all of this."

"Ok, well, tell her we love her and you two be safe, ok?"

"We will, dad. Love you too."

I felt a little guilty lying to them, but it was the only way I could think to make anything better. Based on everything I had seen, they had two to three days left to live. And letting them live out that time thinking everything was going to be alright was the greatest kindness I could give them.

"Hey dad, can you put mom on?" I tried to say as casually as possible.

I took a deep breath and prepared to say goodbye.

I sat on the light brown microsuede love seat in my living room. Normally I chose the couch, but only because it faced the TV. The love seat was barely used so the cushions were still plump and therefore far more comfortable. Since the TV was no longer a factor, I decided this would be my new seat of choice. Plus it was directly across from Shayra's chair and being able to see it made me feel a little better somehow.

I spent the better part of the morning searching my sister's belongings to see if I could find a clue about the password that would finally gain me entry to her laptop. I was already tired from the emotionally draining conversation with my parents, and so I had given up about 12:30 and decided to cook a frozen pizza for lunch before picking up the search again.

For now, I sat staring at the locked computer with a plate of pizza crust next to me, no closer to accessing it than when I had found it in Dr. Gainsborough's office the day before. If only she had been able to tell me the password before she died. Or at least give me some clue as to—

"I don't even know the password!" The words of our last exchange the day before came vividly flooding back.

"Alexander..."

Could it be possible...

I typed "*Alexander*" into the password field and the lock screen instantly disappeared, revealing my sister's not surprisingly well organized desktop.

Is my name everybody's password at Lykos?

I saw instantly what I was looking for. A text document titled "*Alex*" had been placed purposefully in the center of the screen. My hands were shaking as I moved the cursor to open the file.

Alex,

This isn't going to be easy for me to write or, I'm guessing, for you to read. But I have so much I need to say and I don't know how much time I have left, so I'm just going to get straight to the point.

The nano-organisms are airborne, and they are spreading fast. I predict they will have covered the entire planet in the span of a couple of weeks. I have been running experiments and have yet to find a way to stop them that doesn't also harm the host. However, even if I did, their ability to spread and reproduce is beyond anything in the known world, so any attempt to contain them would be completely futile. So far, the only thing that seems to be able to stop them is an airtight seal.

This is the end of the world, Alex. There's no stopping it now. But as dire as the situation seems, there is still hope. Or, at least, something like hope.

As soon as I realized what Dr. Gainsborough was trying to do, I knew we would need to create a contingency plan in case things went south. And so, for the last few weeks, I've been putting together that plan.

I call it "The Rose Contingency."

Give me a break, I didn't really have much time to devote to coming up with a name.

There's a facility in Oklahoma City. A subcontractor of Lykos that has been focusing heavily on cloning for the last decade or so. But the project was abandoned due to "fund reallocation to a more lucrative endeavor." In short, they pulled the funding in favor of Project Nil because they thought the end result would bring in more money. But from what I understand, the project was all but complete, lacking only a final test run using human DNA.

There's even a cryogenic storage unit onsite where they have already gathered the samples. All we need is someone who can start the process and then hang out to monitor it. That's where you come in.

Now I know you well enough to know exactly what you are thinking. You are thinking "Why me?" The answer is easy: there's nobody else on this planet whom I would trust to pull this off. You are more than you believe you are.

However, there is also another reason why it has to be you.

You've probably noticed by now that you are the only one who doesn't seem to be affected by the nano-organisms. I gave the blood you donated to Dr. Gainsborough and he used it as the host to grow them. I had a theory that if things got out of control and they started spreading, they would recognize the DNA of their host and leave it mostly alone. A theory that I confirmed in the lab earlier today. In fact, the rate at which the sample of your blood lost red blood cells was almost identical to the rate at which your body produces new red blood cells. In short, it will be years before you feel any effects.

I know this is probably a little overwhelming, and I wish I didn't have to put this burden on you. But I believe in you, Allie. I've always believed in you.

I told you that I would go broke betting on you if that's what it came to. Well, I'm putting my money where my mouth is. I have bet it all on you. And I don't intend to be wrong about something and break my perfect streak.

It's too late to save the human race, Alex. But it's not too late to give it a second chance. The Rose Contingency can be that second chance. You have to get to that facility and start the incubation process. You are the only one left who can. The Lykos computer network will be in emergency mode, so there is a master override password that will get you into any Lykos system. As you've gained access to this computer, you already know what that password is.

I know you think this is your fault, but it's not. It's not either of our faults. Dr. Gainsborough would have found someone else to do it if I had refused. But placing blame won't help anything now. We can only start from here.

Like I always say, "Tomorrow is a new day, with no mistakes in it."

Now go, Alex. Go and save the world.

I love you.

I wish I had said that more.

-Shay

14

Saturday, April 24th, 2032

Seeing I-30 completely abandoned on a Saturday was an eerily unsettling sight. Nothing but empty lanes at a time when traffic would normally be thick and fast paced. I didn't even bother signaling as I moved one lane to the right to take the Alta Mere exit that looped around the west side of the Ridgemar mall. The pavement changed from a medium gray to a light gray where the exit connected to the main highway. In the past, I had always been too busy watching the other cars on the street to notice.

I had spent the previous day and a half getting ready for my trip to Oklahoma City. I had done laundry, researched anything I could find about a Lykos facility in OKC, packed, and re-read Shayra's letter about a dozen times. The only thing that remained was securing provisions for the trip.

I still couldn't believe what I had read. She had always said she believed in me. In fact, she virtually never stopped saying it. But I had convinced myself that it was just a big sister thing, just something she had to say. In reality, her belief in me was so deep and genuine that she had placed the survival of the entire human race on me. It was a burden I couldn't really wrap my head around yet, but that was probably best. If I started thinking too hard about what was really at stake I would lose my mind.

So instead I focused exclusively on the practical. I was taking a trip to Oklahoma City and I had no reason to think I would be coming back. That meant packing as much as I could fit in my sister's Prius. The Lykos epidemic (I refused to call it by the name they had given it) had hit Fort Worth so unexpectedly that people had little or no time to panic. People in OKC had a little more warning, so I had to assume that every grocery store in the area had been cleaned out, as people tend to do during a crisis. That meant a trip to the local grocery store before leaving town. Without bothering to check if the light was green,

I turned left off of Alta Mere onto Fairchild, the inroad into the empty store parking lot.

It took a little effort to get into the store, but a lug wrench to the front door glass proved to be quite effective. Now, I stood in the soup aisle, trying to decide if ten cans of beef ravioli would cover my needs in the tomato based canned cuisine department, or if it would be wise to include some spaghetti rings to really fill out the menu.

Canned pasta probably wasn't the most weight efficient choice, but without knowing in what state I would find Oklahoma City or how long I would be looking for this cloning facility, I decided to avoid anything that needed to be kept cold or had an otherwise short shelf life. Which, of course, limited my choices considerably. After surveying my basket filled with canned sodas, soups, and about fifteen varieties of potato chips, I decided that the spaghetti rings would be a nice addition to my food choices.

As I gathered the fourth can into my arms, I froze. A distant noise caught my attention. A clicking. Or maybe a tapping. I turned towards the end of the aisle to see if I could spot the source of the noise but saw nothing. Maybe a drip from some kind of leak? Or one of the metal shelves settling under the weight of two hundred pounds of beef ravioli?

But as I was making my analysis, I detected another noise accompanying the first that made my blood run cold. A deep, throaty growl, a few aisles away now and growing steadily louder. I stood frozen in place, all four cans still in my ever tightening grip, watching the end of the aisle and waiting for whatever it was that was inching my way to reveal itself.

As the beast rounded the corner, I immediately noticed the unmistakable pink collar encrusted with rhinestones. It was the neighbor's black lab, Daisy. Or, at least, what she had become. Her usual happy disposition had been replaced with a hunting stance and the tongue that usually hung from her mouth had been replaced by black, lifeless eyes set inches above bared teeth. Teeth that, along with the fur around her mouth, bore a blood red stain.

"Mrs. Hartley..." I whispered, suddenly horrified at the implications.

Without warning, the growl turned to a violent snarl as she suddenly charged towards me. Instinctively I stepped backwards, crashing into the shelf behind me. I tumbled shoulder first to the floor, bringing a dozen or so cans of spaghetti rings down with me. As I rolled quickly to my back and pushed myself to a sitting position, I saw that Daisy was about fifteen feet away and was closing quickly. I reached for something, anything, that I could use to hit her. I kept my eyes fixed on her rapidly approaching form as I groped blindly around the cold floor to my left. Finally my hand came to rest on one of the cans that had accompanied me in my fall. Without hesitating, I launched it forwards, hoping it would at least slow her down and buy me the precious seconds I needed to stand and escape. The can made contact just below her eye, causing her to lose her footing and sending her sliding into the base of the shelf to my right.

That was the chance I was hoping for. I stood quickly and, before she could do the same, reached up and emptied an entire shelf of ravioli onto her head. I turned and ran as fast as I could towards the opposite end of the aisle from where I had first seen her. As I reached it, I turned to see if she had recovered enough to resume the pursuit. She had already stood and had begun attacking one of the cans that had fallen on her head. She whipped it violently back and forth, sending marinara sauce splattering in every direction. That wouldn't keep her busy for long.

I turned forward and evaluated my options. There was no way I was going to outrun her on foot without some kind of distraction. I scanned the shelves in front of me for something that would work. I heard the clanking of cans and the rhythmic tapping of claws on the tile floor behind me just as my eyes landed on the refrigerated meat twenty feet to my left. I ran as fast as I could towards the beef section and picked out the biggest package of steak that I could quickly find. With one hand I grabbed it out of the cooler, and with the other I tore frantically at the plastic wrapping. It finally gave way, spilling the contents on the floor and leaving a trail of raw meat behind me.

That worked. The crazed animal stopped at the first piece of meat and started tearing into it. To celebrate my triumph, I let myself slow down just enough to look back and see how long it would take her to finish the first steak. She had it in her mouth and was whipping it back and forth with unbridled ferocity. But then, to my surprise, she flung it across the aisle and turned her eyes back towards me. She started moving in my direction again, stepping over the other steaks and ignoring them completely. That's when I realized she wasn't hungry at all. She was only interested in the kill.

With a fresh dose of fear and adrenaline, my pace quickened. I knew I had to find some kind of weapon or it would only be a matter of time before she got the best of me. Fifty feet ahead, I spotted the kitchenware aisle and decided that was the only place to look that fit my available time frame.

After what felt more like five hundred feet, I finally reached the end cap. Unfortunately, so did Daisy. She snapped at my foot, missing my heel by mere centimeters. Thankfully my shoes gave me considerably better traction than her paws gave her which allowed me to round the corner onto the aisle with relative ease, while she went sliding past. This afforded me just the time needed to grab the biggest knife I could find and rip off the plastic sheath. I turned to face my attacker just in time to see her hind legs launch her muscular body into the air and directly at me. Her front paws caught me right in the chest, sending me and the knife hurtling to the ground in separate directions. I landed flat on my back and my head bounced sharply off of the hard tile floor. Daisy held her position on my chest, ready to claim her kill, while my hand searched frantically for the knife I had dropped.

As she reared back for the killing blow, my fingers ran across the plastic handle. I gripped it tight and, with all my strength, plunged the blade into the side of her neck. She let out a yelp and recoiled, buying me enough of a window to scoot away and stand to my feet. I turned quickly towards her, ready for the next attack. But instead, she lay motionless on the floor, the plastic knife handle still protruding from the side of her neck. I let out a deep sigh and bent over in exhaustion, resting my weight on my hands just above my knees. As the frenzy of the moment began to settle in my mind and my heartbeat began to return to normal, I forced one more look at Daisy's lifeless body.

How much more death am I going to have to deal with?

If this ordeal had shown me one thing, it was that I definitely needed a way to protect myself. I was reminded of my previous injuries as I pushed myself to an upright position and moved towards the end of the aisle. Each step was a painful struggle. I looked around the store, trying to gain my bearings. Before making my way back to my basket full of food, there was one more department I needed to visit. I turned to the left and begin making my way to sporting goods.

15

After securing a hunting knife and a twelve gauge shotgun with plenty of ammo from sporting goods, I reclaimed my carefully selected rations and I was finally on the road. The drive to Oklahoma City was about three hours and fifteen minutes according to the GPS on my phone and I was nearing the end of hour number two. To say the scenery was unimpressive would be a bit of an understatement. It was mostly barren plains and brush with the occasional barn or grouping of trees. I had just passed the sign that said to take the next exit for the Arbuckle Wilderness Park, which brought with it a flood of memories.

My parents had taken Shayra and me there when we were kids. It was a drive-through safari off of I-35, about halfway between Ardmore and Purcel. You pay some money and they give you cups of food that you can feed to the animals from your car window. At least the more docile and friendly animals, like the goats and gazelles. The animals that they deemed dangerous, like the rhinoceros or the jungle cats, are safely contained for long distance viewing. Shayra spent the entire time telling us the genus and species of every animal we saw, and then mocking me mercilessly when I called the black jaguar a panther.

Normally, I would have considered it unwise to spend so much of a road trip daydreaming, but since I was the only car to be found on I-35, I didn't really feel much need to focus. In fact, I had long given up even trying to stay in just one lane. The monotonous sound of the tires on asphalt and the purr of the Prius's hybrid engine made it easy to get lost in thought.

The interior of the car still smelled like her. It's funny how people tend to have their own unique smell. Some kind of combination of their laundry detergent, shampoo, and the various other scents picked up from the places they spend their time. A sort of aromatic imprint of their life. Shayra always smelled like, among other things, lavender. She said it relaxed her and helped the stress of her job melt away. That was why it was the scent she chose for her car air freshener. Just like everything else she did, it was intentional and practical.

Unlike Charlie, who did most of what she did for only one reason: she wanted to. Consequences were always more of a secondary factor to her. That was part of what drew me to her. Spontaneity. Adventure. It was what my life was lacking. *She* was what my life was lacking. I loved my sister and I loved living with her, but I knew it couldn't last forever. Organizational charts and The Discovery Channel just weren't for me.

Shayra had no interest in dating anyone. She had science and she had me, and that seemed to be all she needed. I guess that's why I had stayed for so long. I didn't want her to be alone. I had convinced myself somehow that she needed me there, even though logically I knew that was ridiculous. She is the most self-sufficient person in the world.

Was the most self-sufficient.

I felt a familiar pang in my stomach as I remembered again that she was gone. I decided to shift my daydreaming to happier things.

Charlie always smelled amazing. A combination of coffee and dragon fruit. She always had a cup of coffee in her hand, and if she didn't, it was because she was on her way to get one. Dragon fruit was her scent of choice for body sprays, air fresheners, and pretty much anything else she could find. I remember how excited she got a couple of years before when it made a big mainstream emergence, a lot like pomegranate did when I was a teenager. She would always drag me to the mall to see—

As I approached the exit sign for US-77, motion in the trees on the side of the road snapped me out of my memories. A fifteen foot wall of rock along the east side of the road blocked the view of the wilderness preserve beyond. The wall sloped downward until it leveled out with the ground right before the sign announcing the impending exit. Just beyond it in the grove of trees, I thought I had seen…something. A shape. A movement of some kind.

I depressed the brake to begin slowing down as I tried to focus in on whatever had caught my eye.

There it was again. This time I was sure of it.

I increased the pressure I was already applying to the brake pedal to bring the car to a complete stop. The unknown perpetrator burst from behind the trees and began to charge at me.

It was a rhinoceros.

A rhinoceros?

“What in the…” I started the sentence but wasn’t about to take the time to finish it.

I grabbed frantically at the gear shift to try and switch the car into reverse, but it was too late. The impact lifted the passenger side of the car and whipped my body uncontrollably from side to side. The sound of metal twisting and glass shattering filled my ears. As the car settled back to the ground, I heard the clatter of my supplies being tossed around inside the cargo area. When the havoc subsided, I shook my head back and forth to break the disorientation. A plume of smoke and a smell like a dirty barbecue grill filled the interior of the car.

Is the car on fire?

I glanced to my left to see if I could pinpoint the origin of the problem. The side impact airbag had deployed, no doubt producing the smoke and the odor. I turned back the other direction to see if I could assess the aftermath of the impact itself. The sharp tip of the creature’s horn had pierced the passenger side front door and was now just inches from the side of my head. I recoiled as far as I could, pressing my back up against the driver side door while pressing my feet against the center console to try and push myself back even further. The rhino kept pushing forward, taking all three thousand pounds of the Prius with it. I twisted my body to try and reach the handle of the door behind me and, in the process managed to jam my elbow into the steering wheel, causing the horn to let out an unexpected honk. That startled the creature enough to make it back off for a moment, unfortunately taking the impaled passenger door with it.

As the door ripped from its hinges, the passenger side of the car lifted about a foot in the air and then bounced back down to the pavement, sending me whipping back and forth a second time. I regained my bearings a little quicker this time and looked towards my attacker. I guessed it had taken the noise of the horn as an act of aggression, because it had made its way about thirty feet from the car and was turning back around, positioning for another attack. It clawed at the ground with its front foot, sending small dust clouds billowing into the air, and shook its head side to side with a grunt.

This was my chance. I turned in my seat towards the steering wheel, reached over and moved the gear selector to the drive position, and stomped the gas pedal to the floor.

No response. The car wasn't moving. I scanned the multiple info screens to see if I could spot the problem, which I did almost instantly.

The car was off. I reached up and pressed the start button as fast as I could, again with no response. I tried a few more times before looking to the right to see that the rhino was now charging towards the vehicle. About thirty feet and closing. With my left hand I grabbed the fold down handle above the driver side window and with my right hand I gripped the seat just below my right thigh, as if either of those contact points would hold me in place for what was coming. Then, I did the only thing I could and braced for impact.

With a crash the horizon began to tilt. I gripped my handholds so tight I could feel my pulse in my fingers. The Prius protested loudly as gravity pulled me toward the driver side window an instant before the side of the car made contact with the pavement. The impact shattered the window, driving bits of glass into the shoulder that had been resting up against it.

I screamed out in pain, as if the rhino would hear me and have some pity. With another crash the horizon went almost completely upside down.

I felt a sharp pain in the back of my head and suddenly all the sounds of metal and glass and the grunting animal began to echo. The shapes around me went blurry and I heard the crack of the Prius's hatchback breaking open just before I lost consciousness.

16

Sunday, April 25th, 2032

I stood about six feet from the hospital bed. The droning, constant squeal of the flatlining heart monitor was the only sound. The air was thick with the smell of lavender. Shayra's body lay in the bed in front of me, a white sheet draped over her and pulled up to just above her waist, leaving the top half of her hospital gown clad body visible.

I started slowly towards the bed, my breathing labored. No code team stood around the bed. No shouts about shocks and compression. No noise of any kind except the relentless tone of the heart monitor. My sister's red hair cascaded perfectly down both sides of the pillow where her head lay and her skin was almost as pale as the sheet that covered her lower half. I stopped a few inches from the bed.

"Shayra," I whispered, not expecting a response.

The tone of the heart monitor was louder now, becoming an almost painful ringing in my ear. As I watched, the walls of the room seemed to fade away, although now I was unsure if they had even been there to begin with.

Without warning, a hand grabbed my wrist. I looked down at my sister's face just in time to see her eyes open abruptly. I tried to recoil but her grip was persistent.

"What have you done?" she whispered fiercely, her voice hoarse. "You've killed them all!"

Finally, I broke free of her grip and turned to run, but instead the floor gave way and I began to fall.

A peppering of dust against the side of my face woke me. Everything was blurry. Everything hurt. The pressure in my head was especially prevalent and there was a throbbing pain on the back side from some presumed point of impact. I reached up to feel the extent of the injury, but when I pulled my hand back all that was present was some flakes of dried blood. Whatever it looked like before, it had already started to heal up.

I looked around to see if I could jog my memory about the events of—Earlier? Yesterday? How long had I been out of it? As my vision began to clear, I saw the dirt and sagebrush of the ground through the cracked windshield above me. Or, perhaps, below me. I checked the rearview mirror and saw nothing but blue sky and wispy clouds.

It was daytime. That was the first real fact I was able to establish about the situation. Quickly after, I was able to surmise that the Prius, while still upside down, was now resting mostly on its nose. The growing awareness of a persistent pain in my waist told me that my seatbelt was the reason that I had remained in my seat, thus accompanying the vehicle to its inverted position.

Without thinking I reached down and depressed the release on my restraint, giving gravity the opportunity to fold me in half and wedge my contorted form between the roof of the car and the steering wheel.

After a few minutes of comedic struggle, I managed to crawl out the passenger side of the car, which was made much easier by the gaping hole left by the missing door. With some difficulty, I stood and stepped back far enough to take in the whole scene.

The Prius, now mostly unrecognizable as such, was not going to be taking me anywhere else. The side I had escaped from had been smashed and impaled multiple times, the hatchback lid had been completely demolished, and at least one of the wheels had been removed and was nowhere in sight. The food I had stowed in the cargo area now littered the ground around the back end of the vehicle. Every bit that hadn't been carried off had been trampled into the dirt. The shotgun appeared to still be in good shape, but I could see no sign of the hunting knife or most of the shotgun ammo.

I reached for my phone, which I had recovered from the center console on the way out. It still seemed to be in working order, though the battery level was down to nine percent. Before I could unlock it to check my GPS, the date and time caught my attention.

12:54 p.m. Sunday, April 25th

I had been out for almost twenty-four hours. I hung my head and squeezed my eyes shut as this new bit of information set in.

That had to be the worst part of all of this. The uncontrollable thoughts. The unrelenting guilt. Every new turn of events brought with it fresh realizations of death and helplessness. Unconscious for twenty-four hours, and all I could think of was how many people had died during that time period. People I knew. People I hated. People I loved—

I made myself stop there. I had almost no confidence that I could actually pull this off and falling apart was only going to make it worse. Each time I had to push my emotions aside, it was just a little bit easier. I hated that. The people I cared about deserved better. They deserved my grief. It was only right.

But for the time being, the only tribute I could offer for them was a refusal to quit. The Rose Contingency had to be everything right now.

I unlocked my phone, opened the GPS app, and resumed the course to Oklahoma City. The time to destination showed an hour and eighteen minutes. That was, of course, if I had a vehicle, which I did not. I tapped the icon of the little man at the bottom of the screen next to the car icon to change from driving directions to walking. The time changed to one day and five hours.

Crap.

Twenty-nine hours of walking and not a scrap of food for the trip. That was not exactly an ideal ratio. I switched to the satellite imagery view and used my fingers to zoom in on the surrounding area to check for any other options.

There was some kind of visitor's center on the far side of the wildlife preserve, but trying to make it there without knowing the state of the park or, more importantly, the state of the animals in the park, didn't seem like a very prudent choice.

I continued moving the map view around to see what was nearby. North of the wilderness park, and just on the other side of a creek that ran along the side of the road, was a small complex with one big building and twelve smaller buildings a little ways down a dirt path. I tapped on the larger building and a label appeared, announcing that I had discovered Deer Creek Cabins and Lodge. I guessed the smaller buildings were individual cabins that could be rented. Places like that were not usually kept stocked with any kind of food, so that didn't really help me. The main lodge, however, most likely contained, at the very least, some vending machines.

I tucked my phone in my pocket and turned towards the remains of the Prius to also retrieve my shotgun and the few intact shells I could locate. Just in case.

17

Making my way across the creek and over to the Deer Creek Lodge turned out to be the easiest task I had undertaken on this trip so far. The front door was even unlocked. Had I not been so excited to finally encounter some good fortune, I probably would have been much more leery of an unsecured door at an empty facility. However, even in my excitement I proceeded slowly. I sidestepped cautiously through the door, locking it behind me and pushing it closed until I heard it latch. I was already going over in my mind the motion that would be needed to get the shotgun that was now strapped to my back into a fireable position.

The lodge seemed to be in perfect shape, apart from being unoccupied. That was the strangest part of the apocalypse: it was so subtle. There was no zombie hordes, no desolated cities, no modern ruins reclaimed by years of unchecked overgrowth. At least, not yet. Instead, everyone was simply dying in their beds, mostly unaware of how little time they had left. The human race, disappearing quietly into oblivion with not so much as a struggle.

The only real indicator that anything was amiss in the lodge was the air. It was thick and humid with a stale scent that I couldn't quite place. A few specks of dust, stirred up by my disturbing of the recently untouched front door, drifted slowly through the beams of light shining in through the nearby window. The way they hung in the air told me there was little to no air flow in the room. Whoever was the last one out the door had shut off the AC. And possibly everything else.

The lobby of the Deer Creek Lodge was hauntingly quiet. Just inside the door to the left was the front desk. A dormant computer monitor sat alone at one end and a rack full of brochures sat on the opposite. Neatly arranged pamphlets advertised the Arbuckle wilderness park and various other tourist attractions in the OKC area like Frontier City and the Overholser Mansion.

Across the room on the north wall was an understated sitting area. A couple of arm chairs and a wooden table with magazines fanned out purposefully in the center. Just beyond the table was a fireplace, which I guessed hadn't been used in months, and mounted to the wall above it was a pair of antlers that seemed to me far too large and symmetrical to be real. The light from the window cast the long, harsh shadow of the antlers across the entire north-west corner of the otherwise dark room. It was beautiful in its own way, but not beautiful enough for me to linger.

After a preliminary scan of the room, I spotted a back hallway in the west corner, just on the other side of the staircase. That path seemed like the most promising to lead me to some vending machines. A few feet down from the lobby, I spotted my quarry in a small alcove just off of the main hallway. Three machines lined the wall inside with an ice maker in the far corner, bottled soft drinks in the middle and, just inside the doorway, a machine containing various chips and snack cakes. The front side of that machine was mostly made of glass, so I guessed one good blow from the butt of my shotgun would open the way to a bounty of replacement rations.

I reached back to move the weapon into place, but stopped mid-movement when I felt an unknown object press firmly and abruptly into the middle of my back. Slowly, I tried turning to identify whatever it was that was poking in my back and, more importantly, the animal or person who held it there, but a gruff southern voice caused me to freeze again.

"Don't move boy, or it'll be the last mistake ya make, I tell ya."

"I'm sorry," I started as I moved my hands above my head to indicate my surrender, "I really didn't think anybody would be here."

"So I guess ya thought ya could just take whatever ya want then, eh?"

"No, not...well...not really. I'm on my way to Oklahoma City and my car got destroyed. All my food too. I just needed some food for the trip because now I have to walk the rest of the way..."

"Ya sure do talk a lot, boy," he interrupted. "Turn around now. Nice and slow."

I did as he asked, keeping my hands lifted above my head. As I completed my turn I saw an older black man standing in front of me pointing some sort of small caliber rifle at my chest. His grip on the weapon seemed almost awkward, but it had a certain precision to it that only comes with experience. I guessed he was in his late sixties or early seventies, with short white hair and what appeared to be a couple weeks growth of white stubble on his face. He looked me thoroughly up and down.

"Ya don't look like a looter," he said, relaxing the position of his gun by a couple of inches.

"I'm really not," I insisted.

I saw a subtle change in his face, as though he had just noticed something.

"What's ya name, son?" he asked.

"Alexander Lee."

"Lee? Are ya related to that scientist who let this sickness loose on everybody?"

I dropped my hands and took a step towards him.

"She did not—" I started aggressively before he raised the rifle barrel back to its previous position, causing me to put a little more thought into my next words.

"It wasn't her fault," I tried again.

He watched me suspiciously, still waiting for the answer to his question.

"And yes," I added, "she was my sister."

That seemed to be enough to spark some sort of compassion in him. Or at least pity. He lowered the gun to his side and stared at me for a moment.

"I see," he said finally.

He seemed almost as relieved as I was that he was no longer pointing the rifle at my heart. He relaxed his right leg just enough to allow him to lean against the door frame. The stern look faded from his face and something else took its place. Something I had already seen on more faces than I cared to revisit. He was infected, and if I had to guess, he didn't have long. And yet, he was here, still standing and strong enough to defend his...whatever this place was to him. Workplace, maybe?

He was definitely sick, but somehow he was alive and, as far as I could tell, he was the last one in this area who still was. Before I could ask him how, a quizzical look swept over his face as he looked me up and down a second time. It would seem he was having a similar internal dialogue concerning my equally enigmatic existence.

"Ya don't look sick," he said, almost sounding annoyed by that fact.

"Um, yeah. I'm not, really."

"How come?"

"I'm, uh, kind of immune."

That got his attention.

"Ya what?"

"Well, not really immune. It still effects me. Just…slower."

He stared at me in disbelief for what felt like ten solid minutes.

"So bein' the only one on the planet not dyin' right now, ya thought that the best way to make use of that opportunity is to get ya some dang Cheetos? What in Sam Hill is wrong with you?"

That was not exactly the perspective I was expecting and it took me a moment to pull together a coherent response.

"I'm not...you just...I..." was about all I could manage at first.

He cocked his head to the side, as if daring me to try and formulate a sufficient answer. I closed my eyes and tried one more time to compose myself.

"Look," I asserted, "it's like I told you. I'm on my way to Oklahoma City. I wrecked my car so I have to walk and I need food for the trip. That's all."

"Why?"

"What?"

"Why ya goin' to Oklahoma City?"

"It's kind of a long story," I hesitated.

"Well then, best I can figure I got about nine hours left to live." He stood up straight and motioned back towards the lobby. "So I reckon ya better talk fast."

18

The stranger and I sat in the arm chairs in the lobby of the Deer Creek Lodge, just in front of the dormant fire place. I had just finished giving him a summarized version of my mission and was waiting for his response. He looked unimpressed to say the least. His left elbow sat on the armrest of the chair while he supported his chin with the palm of his left hand. His right leg was crossed over his left, pulling parts of his pants legs tight and betraying his thin, boney frame.

"So you're gonna save the world, huh?" he said finally with a smile.

"Uh, yeah, I guess that's the idea."

After a few more seconds, his smile erupted into a chuckle.

"Saving the world from Lykos," he added with mocking triumph as his chuckle began to build until it was a full blown laugh.

"Um," I started at a volume that I hoped could be heard over his laughter, "why is that funny?"

That didn't help. By now he was bent over forward in a high-pitched guffaw. I shook my head in frustration and waited for it to pass. After about forty-five seconds he had settled back into a light chuckle that finally ended with a sigh. I looked at him impatiently, but he just smiled back at me.

"I remember bein' young like you," he finally explained.

"I'm thirty-two," I contested.

"Not in ya head, ya not."

I almost rolled my eyes at him, but stopped myself. Mainly because I felt that it would only confirm his point.

"I used to work for Lykos, you know?" he said.

That caught me off guard a little. I never would have guessed it based on the man sitting across from me now. I felt an excitement rise up in me. Maybe he knew my sister. Maybe he had stories about her. Somehow it felt like if I could get a glimpse into a moment I didn't already know about, a new moment, it would be almost like she was still here creating moments. I knew it was a ridiculous thought, and yet sitting there in the musty half-light of the Deer Creek Lodge, it was all I could think about.

"You what?" I responded finally.

"Yeah, up till 'bout twelve years ago. Ya remember when they were looking for that cure for leukemia in 2020? That was one of the last projects I worked on before I left."

My heart sank a little. If he was there twelve years ago then he wouldn't have known Shayra. Even still, this was still sounding increasingly familiar. My sister was talking about Lykos and their accomplishments for years before she ever got the internship.

"So what happened?" I asked. "Why did you leave?"

His smile disappeared. He turned his head and gazed blankly into the empty fireplace to his left. After a few contemplative moments he spoke.

"When I started at Lykos I was convinced that I was goin' to save the world." The slightest smile returned to his lips as he turned and nodded in my direction. "Just like you."

I straightened in my chair out of reflex, unaware that I was slouching until that moment.

"But it didn't take long to figure out that Gainsborough didn't have the same goal. He wanted money and recognition. 'To be remembered in the annals of history' is how he put it. Science was only a means to an end for him."

"But your team cured leukemia," I argued. "That's something scientists had been trying to do for two hundred years."

"We did. And then they slapped a price tag on it. Ya know how much that treatment cost without insurance? Two hundred and forty grand. People still die from leukemia every day just 'cause they can't afford the cure. Turns out, no matter how many people want to help others, there's always somebody there to collect the profits for their work."

I opened my mouth to speak, but couldn't think of anything that could undo his point. I lowered my head and stared at the floor. Shayra believed like the stranger used to. Even in her last moments, she still believed that she could use science to do some good.

We sat in silence for a long while before he finally spoke again.

"Yep, every young scientist believes they're gonna save the world." He looked slowly across the empty expanse of the lodge, seemingly taking in its haunting state. "But, ya know, I really thought Shayra just might actually do it."

My head shot up at the mention of my sister's name. "Wait...you knew her?"

He smiled slightly once more. "After I left Lykos, I got a spot teachin' biochemistry at OSU. Your sister was in my class my second semester there. She was brilliant. Ten times smarter than I could ever be. She made me realize that I had nothin' left to offer the scientific community. She was supposed to be the student, but she was the one teachin' me things. So I left and came here. Well, to Arbuckle, actually."

I mulled over his story for a moment. Something about all this still sounded familiar. Like a distant memory from some late night conversation over coffee. Suddenly it clicked.

"Wait…Wilson? You're Patrick Wilson?"

"Patrick is good enough, but yeah, that's me. I take it she mentioned me?"

"Of course! She told me about your team and their work with leukemia and how you—" I hesitated as the memory completed itself in my mind. "You got her the internship at Lykos."

The somber look in his eyes told me he understood the implications of that. He shifted slightly in his chair.

"I did. I called Gainsborough and I told him that she was the most gifted scientist I had ever seen and if he didn't bring her on, then somebody else would. I told him that she—"

"She what?" I asked impatiently.

"That she was gonna make a lotta money for somebody, so it might as well be him."

I leaned back in my chair. I tried to make my disapproval clear by my expression, but he had already looked away.

"I was just tryna speak his language. I thought she could make a real difference. Be a hero, ya know? But now, they've made her out to be the villain."

"And you feel like you're to blame for that?"

"Who else is there?"

"Gainsborough. He pushed her to do the tests even after she told him they weren't safe."

"Of course he did. People like him will always make others do their dirty work. You can't stop there from bein' bad people in the world. All you can do is make sure you ain't one of them. I left Lykos so I wouldn't become a villain like them. But then I sent ya sister in there to fix what I couldn't. To do *my* dirty work. So in the end, how am I any better than them?"

I listened in silence. I knew I had a scowl on my face by now but I saw no reason to try and hide my displeasure with him. Why was he telling me all this? Was I supposed to comfort him?

"What am I supposed to say to that?" I asked, irritated. "Do you want me to try and make you feel better?"

He chuckled again which only irritated me more. I leaned forward in my chair into more of a confrontational position.

"Oh, it's too late for that," he said as he also leaned forward and his smile disappeared again. "I know what I did. I sent that poor girl to her death."

His bluntness threw me. "Ok. So what's the point of telling me all of this?"

"I'm tryna warn ya, Alex. So many villains start out tryna save the world. You have no idea what it can turn ya into."

19

Three beef patties crackled and sizzled in the metal skillet. Steam rose up from the cooking surface and drifted into the industrial vent hood above. It was the most amazing smell I could remember ever smelling. I hadn't eaten a real meal since the fish tacos I had the night Shayra called to tell me she was in the hospital. That night seemed like a lifetime ago and I couldn't even wrap my head around the fact that it had actually only been five days before. The world had changed so much, and yet it hadn't. Every building stood exactly where it had, but now abandoned. Completely devoid of human touch, but still mostly dusted and vacuumed. The well kept state of everything served as a vivid reminder of just how fresh the apocalypse really was. Even the normalcy of watching Patrick flip a hamburger in a skillet was uncharacteristically unsettling.

“Ever been?” he said.

I shook my head to dispel the daydream. I had allowed my thoughts to drift off while watching him cook. I paused to try and retrace the conversation. He had offered me a hamburger. I had asked for two. He had retrieved the meat from the walk in fridge of the Deer Creek Lodge kitchen and then grabbed a skillet from the wall rack before cranking up the burner on the commercial grade stove. Then I had asked how he was still alive when everyone else in this area had already died.

That was it. That was the story he was telling me.

“Um, no. No I haven’t. Is it nice?” I tried.

“Oh yeah. I mean, it’s pretty cold for most of the winter but about this time of year it starts gettin’ tolerable. Anyway, I got a cabin I built right there on Lake Nipigon, up on the northwest side right ‘round the Windigo Bay area. There’s just enough flatland right there to land my Cessna.”

I did a quick search on my phone while he spoke to see if I could fill in the gaps that I had missed while daydreaming. The results quickly told me that Lake Nipigon was in Ontario.

"So you were in Canada when all this started?" I responded, as if I had heard him say that himself minutes before.

"Yeah, that's what I said. Anyway, I guess I was out there in the middle of nowhere so it took awhile to get to me. I didn't start feeling sick until last night. I knew it was what everybody was gettin' so I figured if I was gonna die then I wanted to die at home, you know? So I flew back to OKC early this mornin'."

"So why did you come out here?"

"I heard what they were sayin about all the animals goin' nuts and all." He nudged the hamburger patties around in the skillet while he spoke. "Well, I used to work here, ya know? I've known a lot of these animals since they were born."

"So you came to see if it was true?" I said solemnly.

I had a pretty good idea where this story was going to end up.

"Yeah. There was a, uh, a black jaguar here. I was there when she was born. We were pretty close. I just knew she'd recognize me."

"And?"

He didn't answer at first, but rather stared down at the skillet. I noticed he had stopped fiddling with the meat and his grip on the spatula had tightened.

"I had to put her down," he said finally.

After a moment he went back to mindlessly nudging the patties. I wasn't sure how to respond to that. The pain of loss had become such commonplace to the few of us who remained alive, any condolence was beginning to lose its meaning.

"I'm sorry," was the only response I could manage.

The words felt as painfully normal as the recently dusted lodge. And just as empty. He cleared his throat.

"Don't matter," he said briskly. "I guess we'll all be dead 'for long."

He placed my two hamburger patties on the buns that were open and waiting on a plate next to the stove and then he pushed it in my direction. After I took it from his hand, he went through the same process with his burger and then turned to walk back towards the chairs in the lobby.

"What was her name?" I asked as he reached the door.

He turned and paused for a moment. He let out a chuckle, but I saw his eyes glistening in the dim light of the kitchen.

"We called her Shelly," he said.

A knowing smile crossed my lips. "I lost a Shelly too."

He nodded and then turned back towards the lobby. Normalcy had become an unsettling reminder of the state of the world. The exchange we shared, with its mixture of levity and grief and comparing the names of the ones we had lost, was strange. Just strange enough to be comforting.

"So, why didn't you go back home after…all that?" I asked as delicately as I could.

He wiped his hands with a white paper napkin before tossing it onto his empty plate.

"I was fixin' to. But by the time I got back to my truck them blasted chimps had torn it apart."

"Chimps?" I asked in surprise. "As in, chimpanzees?"

"Yeah, them fellas have gone nuts. They had a habitat over on the north side of the park but they broke out and just started wreckin' everything. I made my way across the park and over here to the lodge. I was checkin the rations in the kitchen when I heard ya come in. I thought it was them apes again."

"Well," I chuckled, "based on how you greeted me it sounds like they're lucky they stayed away."

We both laughed just enough to bring the conversation to a lull. We sat in the reflective silence for a few minutes before Patrick broke it again.

"So, how about you?"

"How about me what?"

"Well, we talked about me plenty. But I bet ya lost a few people too. I mean, besides ya sister, of course."

I shifted in my seat a little. "Uh, yeah. A few, I guess."

"So go on then!" he barked.

I was briefly taken aback at his tone. We had been having such a civil conversation I had forgotten how abrupt and gruff he was when we first met.

"Um, ok, I guess. Well, there's my parents. They live in New York but they're on vacation in New Mexico right now. They—" I stopped as my heart sank. The timeline hadn't occurred to me until that moment. "They, uh, probably died while I was unconscious in the car."

"Tell me about them." His voice had softened again.

"My dad worked for The New York Post. And my mom didn't work. Not outside the house anyway. They were great. The best, actually."

I reached up to wipe away a tear that was creeping down my cheek toward the weeks worth of stubble on my chin.

"Ok. Who else?"

"Why?" I said with a sniffle. "Why are you making me talk about all this?"

He smiled compassionately. "What else is there? Loss is all we got left."

I sighed. He was right. I had been given this crazy opportunity to have one last human conversation in the middle of the end of the world. I probably shouldn't waste it.

"Yeah, I guess so," I swallowed hard before continuing. "There's Charlie. She was my ex-fiancé."

"Oh? And what happened to her?"

"She...I uh, I don't know, actually. I haven't talked to her in months."

"So, in ya head, she's still alive?"

"She's not. She can't be. I'll probably never know what happened to her."

I could feel my tone sharpening. There was no point in talking about this anymore. I stood and picked up my phone off of the table.

"Thank you for the burgers and everything. But I have to go. I have to find a car of some kind. I have to get to Oklahoma City. And I don't really have time to sit and—"

I froze. A familiar vibrating pattern in my hand shattered my train of thought. It had been days since I had felt it, but I knew instantly what it signified. Someone had sent me a text message. It took me a moment to summon the courage to see who it was from and what it said. Normally, a text was a common occurrence and didn't usually contain anything earth shattering. But the reality I was now living was far outside the bounds of normal.

After a few moments of uncertainty, I finally raised my phone to determine the identity of the sender. I almost dropped my phone in surprise as I read the name.

It was from Charlie.

As I reached my thumb towards the notification to open the message, the screen went black.

20

"Charlie!" I turned frantically to look at Patrick. "That was from Charlie!"

"The girl you was just talking about?" he asked. "What'd it say?"

"I…I don't know. My phone died. Do you have a charger?"

He shrugged. Of course he didn't have one. I hadn't once seen him looking at a cell phone. I patted my pockets for a charging cable, hoping just maybe I hadn't left it in the Prius. No such luck.

I sank back down into the chair as I absorbed this new bit of information. Charlie was alive. But how? Where could she be? At this point, I guessed the only place the nano-organisms hadn't reached was the opposite side of the planet. Maybe Russia? Or India? When she said she wanted to move out of the city, I guess she really meant it.

"I have to go," I resolved. "I have to find a charger."

"What about saving the world?" he asked, almost sarcastically.

"I don't know. That can wait." I turned and looked him square in the eye. I'd never been more sure of anything. "I have to see her one more time."

"Haven't ya been listening to the news? Everybody in the states is dead. If she's alive it means she's thousands of miles away."

"I don't care. I have to try."

As I turned to leave, I felt his hand on my arm. His hold was weak and unpersuasive. I started to pull away but felt his grip tighten and his weight pulling me down. He wasn't trying to stop me. He was using me for balance as he began to fall. I turned and caught him as he all but collapsed against my chest. He reached his arm up around my shoulder and I helped him back up to a standing position.

"Patrick, are you ok?" I asked, already knowing the answer.

"I'm fine, I'm fine," he assured me through gritted teeth.

He released his grip on me and attempted to stand on his own. He was a little unsteady at first, but after just a moment his stance became solid again.

"Alex, ya got a job to do," he protested. "What about The Rose Contingency?"

I stared at him in disbelief. "You laughed at me when I told you about that."

"Yeah, I did. It's a one in a million shot but…"

"But what?" I pressed.

"Your sister was the smartest person I have ever met. If she really believed that this plan…that *you* can save the world…" He took a deep breath. "Then so do I."

I'm not generally a hugger, but in that moment it seemed the only proper response. I wrapped my arms around him so tight he let out an involuntary grunt. I released my embrace gently to prevent him from losing his balance again.

"Thanks, Patrick." I turned to walk away, still a little unsure of what course of action I was going to take.

He was right. If she was alive, that meant she had to be thousands of miles away. On a different continent, most likely. Even if I could get to her, at most she had forty-eight hours. But most probably, she had even less. Would spending that time together really make anything easier? Could anything do that at this point?

No, it couldn't. But even so, I refused to let one more person slip away without so much as a goodbye. I had to at least talk to her. Maybe that would just have to be enough.

"Um," I started as I spun back towards Patrick, "the cloning facility in Oklahoma City. Shayra didn't mention a location."

"No," he shook his head, "I don't suppose she would have. Most people at Lykos didn't even know about that project, much less where to find it."

"Do you know where it is?"

"No, I don't. But maybe…" He paused thoughtfully. "I wonder if that's what they set up in that old museum."

Before he could finish, a loud metallic crash from the kitchen arrested both of our attention.

Patrick swung around and had his rifle in firing position before I could open my mouth.

"What was that?" I asked.

"It's them chimps." His grip on his weapon tightened as he slowly stepped towards the reception desk and the hallway beyond it that lead to the kitchen. “Run, Alex.”

“Patrick, they’re just monkeys,” I reasoned.

But even as I said the words, I had already began stepping backwards towards the front door of the lodge. He turned and looked at me with terror in his eyes.

“No, they’re not. Not anymore. I’ve never seen behavior like this. They’re not hungry or scared. They’re killin’ and destroyin’ because it’s all that’s left in their heads.” He turned back towards the hallway. “They’d just as soon tear you and me apart as they did my truck.”

“I can help!” I insisted as I reached for the shotgun strapped to my back.

He turned the barrel of his gun towards me.

“Go,” he ordered.

That was all the motivation I needed. I turned around just in time to see one of the chimps swing down from the porch roof and land on the concrete outside. It snarled at me through the glass panels on the door before grabbing the handle and violently jerking it in every direction. Fortunately, I had the presence of mind to lock the door behind me when I had first arrived.

Without warning, it let out a deranged sounding howl and punched its fist through the window pain nearest the latch. Blood dripped from its arm as it reached blindly through the broken glass and began groping for the inside doorknob. But even that didn't seem to slow it down, instead it kept its eyes fixed on me and continued snarling. The sounds it made were unnatural, almost otherworldly even. Red tinted saliva splattered in every direction as the animal convulsed in a crazed fit of rage.

I turned back towards Patrick and, behind him, the hallway that lead to the vending machines. That was my only way out. The first chimp leapt from the doorway behind reception and landed on all fours on top of the desk. He pounded his fists into the wood before letting out a chilling cry. It was now or never.

I ran towards the northwest corner of the room, and the hallway there that hopefully led to an outside door, as Patrick fired off a shot. The first chimp collapsed as three more emerged from the hallway to take its place. The front door of the lodge broke open with a crack, followed quickly by the sound of Patrick chambering another round. Just as I reached the back hallway, he took his next shot. The room erupted into deafening chatter, almost drowning out the sound of him loading another round into the chamber.

As I rounded the corner into the hallway, I heard Patrick's voice.

"Let go of that!" he yelled. "Hey! Give me that! No, no, NO—"

The sound of a single rifle blast silenced his cries. I faltered a little bit, but I wouldn't let myself stop. Every muscle burned as I ran. Every impulse in my head was screaming to go back and save him. But I knew it was too late. Just like everyone else, he was gone.

Everyone but Charlie.

I held on to that thought and let it drive me on. Just as the chimps rounded the corner into the hallway behind me, I burst through the door at the end and into the sunlight beyond.

21

Finding a vehicle was my first priority once I emerged from the dark of the lodge. That is, after blocking the door to prevent the chimps from following me outside. I managed to accomplish said task by pushing a half full metal drum of industrial degreaser in front of it.

After a moment, my eyes adjusted to the sun, allowing me to plan my next move. To the north of the main lodge, a dirt and gravel road led to several individual cabins. A dozen or so small structures lined the right side of the road opposite a line of trees on the left, giving the cabins a feeling of seclusion from the main road that was just a few feet on the other side of the tree line. The cabins were separated into groups of four with a grove of trees between each group. Just beyond the first grove, I saw the back end of a black SUV parked outside of one the cabins.

The wave of chimps broke against the inside of the door behind me with a crash and a clamor of chattering and howling. My makeshift barricade wouldn't hold them for long. I took off running as fast as my aching body would let me.

Within a few seconds I had reached the vehicle. The dusty black Range Rover sat on the dirt driveway of cabin six. With any luck, I would find the keys inside. Thanks to the lessons I learned at Dr. Gainsborough's office, it only took one attempt to force my way in. As the door broke open, a smell like rotting cabbage and mothballs assaulted my senses. I felt my gag reflex kick in and I instinctively covered my nose with my shirt. I recognized the smell fairly quickly. I had smelled something similar at Lab D, although there it was mostly covered by the smell of a powerful disinfectant.

It was the smell of death. Something, or more likely someone, had died here. I knew my stomach couldn't handle much more of the putrid scent, so I looked quickly for a set of keys, which I spotted at once on the kitchen island. As I stepped towards it, the smell intensified. On the other side of the island, a shape inching into view caught my attention; An amorphous mound covered by white cloth with tiny blue flowers all over it. I snatched the keys and turned a callused shoulder to the body on the floor. I didn't care to see any more. I couldn't care.

Back outside, the door of the Range Rover unlocked automatically as my fingers touched the handle. I climbed in and pressed the start button.

I wonder who she was?

I shook it off as the engine roared to life. I didn't have time to think about it. Keeping my foot on the brake, I put the vehicle in reverse and then checked the center console to see if there was anything helpful. A white charging cable lay coiled up inside, with one end inserted into a USB power outlet.

I plugged my phone in and waited for it to power up. A loud thud on the hood of the vehicle served me notice that I had lingered longer than I should have.

I looked up to see one of the enraged chimpanzees standing just on the other side of the windshield. It saw me as well and let out a crazed howl. It grabbed ahold of both windshield wipers, one in each hand, and tore them from their mounts before throwing them about twenty feet away. With another howl, it reared back to smash its hands through the glass.

"Not this time," I said to myself.

I slammed the accelerator to the floor, sending the chimp tumbling off of the hood as the vehicle lurched backwards. A cloud of dust and the sound of gravel peppering the Range Rovers undercarriage filled the air.

I came to a stop facing north on the dirt road in front of the cabins and shifted the vehicle immediately into drive. Before I could move, three more chimps jumped up and grabbed onto the outside of the vehicle. Simply accelerating down the road in front of me didn't really seem like a viable option. I could only imagine the damage they could do before I could get up enough speed to throw them off.

Instead, I turned the wheel sharply to the left, heading towards the line of trees on the side of the road opposite the cabins. I sped towards a gap between two of the smaller trees. It looked just big enough for the SUV to fit through and I hoped the branches would knock the apes loose. However, as I approached the gap, my confidence in the vehicle's ability to pass through began to wain. For a moment, I considered abandoning the half-baked plan altogether, but then I would have to find a different way to deal with the creatures, and there wasn't exactly time to sit and weigh the options.

Against my instincts, I pressed the accelerator the rest of the way to the floor. If I couldn't stop, maybe I could get enough speed to squeeze through the space that was now feeling increasingly inadequate.

At the last second, I closed my eyes. The sound of branches breaking, metal creaking, and primates howling filled my ears for the briefest moment before it fell away. I opened my eyes to find that I was traveling the brief open expanse between the line of trees opposite the cabins and the highway. I checked the vehicle to see if I could surmise my results.

My maneuver had been successful in removing all the chimps, as well as both side mirrors, from the outside of the SUV. In my rear view mirror I could see the two trees pushed aside where I had squeezed between them. Most of the branches were broken or missing, leaving a clean gap in the wake of where I had passed through. I leaned back in my seat and let out a deep breath that I hadn't realized until that moment that I had been holding in.

The vehicle had taken a beating but still seemed to be in good working order, minus the sideview mirrors and windshield wipers. The mirrors were mostly useless without other cars on the road anyway, so as long as it didn't rain I would still be in good shape.

A wooden fence and a line of tall grass separated the expanse where I currently was from the pavement of the highway, but the Range Rover didn't care. With one more crash I broke through the fence and burst through the grass onto I-35, leaving shattered wood and splinters in my wake.

As soon as the vehicle tires hit the asphalt, I remembered the text from Charlie. I fumbled to open the lid of the center console to retrieve my phone and see what she had said.

"*Alex?*" the message read simply.

There was far too much to say to just send a text, so instead I tapped on her name at the top of the screen to initiate a phone call. But after four rings, it went to her voicemail.

"Hey, it's Charlie. You can leave a message if you want but let's be real—"

I tapped end before the recording could finish. Had something happened to her? Had she had a similar animal run-in like the ones I had been dealing with? I shut my imagination down before it could get away from me and decided the best course of action was to respond via text then put it out of my mind, at least until I got to Oklahoma City.

"*Are you ok?*" was the only response I could come up with.

As I dropped my phone in the cup holder to allow it to charge, raindrops began to pepper the windshield.

22

The rain made for a slow trip into OKC with no windshield wipers on the Range Rover. It stretched what should have been just over an hour long trip into about three and a half hours. It was just a few minutes after 8:00 p.m. and the sun was already beginning to set when I finally entered the city limits. I had only just reached Oklahoma City, but it had felt like I had been back in civilization for about twenty miles. I had already passed a Cracker Barrel, a Best Buy, and countless car dealerships. Coming into the city from the south brought me through Norman and Moore which, even though they were technically separate cities, were more or less all connected.

Now that I was finally here, I wasn't really sure where to start looking for the cloning facility. Patrick's vague mention of a Lykos facility that had possibly been located in an old museum was all the information I had to go on. I picked up my phone, which was now fully charged, and opened the maps app.

The search for museums in the area yielded about thirty results. Starting at the top of the list and working my way down seemed like the most organized method of working through them all. However, it would have included a substantial amount of backtracking. Maybe starting with the most popular one and then working outward from there would be more efficient.

I was considering these options when the maps app on my screen fell away, replaced by an incoming phone call. The name of the caller barely had time to register in my brain before I tapped the accept button.

"Charlie?" I answered, foregoing any kind of proper greeting.

"Alex!" came her excited response. "You're ok! You *are* ok, right?"

"Yeah, I'm fine. Are you ok?"

"Yeah, I'm good." But even as she said it, I could hear her voice breaking. "Oh God, Alex. I can't believe this is happening. I haven't talked to anybody in days. Everything online was saying that the entire US population had been wiped out and then my phone died and then I finally found a charger and now nobody is saying anything. It's like the whole world has just gone dark—"

"Charlie," I interrupted, "we're alive. That's what's important right now. You and me are gonna figure this out, ok?"

She paused for a moment and I could hear her take a deep breath.

"Ok," she responded with an exhale.

Charlie was the kind of girl who seemed to be in control in every situation. Nothing caught her off guard or rattled her. Hearing her freak out was unsettling, but somehow also made me strangely calm. For the first time since this endeavor started, I felt at least a little confidence in the way I was handling myself.

"First things first," I continued, "where are you?"

"AllianceHealth. It closed down a few years ago but there's an old quarantine wing here."

"AllianceHealth? But isn't that in—"

My heart leapt when she finished my sentence. "Oklahoma City."

AllianceHealth Deaconess was a small hospital on the northwest side of OKC, just south of Lake Hefner. Charlie had worked there as a nurse's assistant for several years before she moved to Fort Worth. It had closed down just a few years before due to, I guessed, the emergence of more affordable urgent care centers in the area and the fact that the larger Integris Baptist Medical Center was less than a mile away on the other side of the highway.

It was a mostly plain red brick building that stood three stories high in the front with a section at the back that stood an additional three stories high. Patient rooms, if I had to guess.

I turned left off of Portland Avenue into the driveway just past the entrance marked for ambulance drop off, as per Charlie's instructions. The sign I passed as I entered indicated I had located parking lot C. I parked the Range Rover under the covered driveway in front of the door and made my way inside.

I had told Charlie that I needed to hang up so I could focus on my route into the city, but in reality that was only about half of the reason. I also needed time to prepare myself. I hadn't seen her in over six months and I didn't even know what to say when I did, given the current conditions.

Should I open with a joke? Walk in there like her savior and declare "Never fear! I will rescue you!" as if I could actually stop anything from hurting her? Maybe a simple "Hello" would suffice.

As I reached the sign for the quarantine wing, my heart began to race. I could see the edge of her shadow through the glass on the third door. The faces of the rooms were made of windows with one door in the middle. The glass was broken up into large triangle sections that were separated by thick white plastic cross bars.

I inched forward slowly, not out of fear of danger, but fearing I wasn't ready for this interaction. At the end of the world, what could I really say? How could I talk casually about our past when the future was so uncertain?

She stood at the door, watching me approach. She wore black leggings and an oversized grey sweatshirt. I recognized it as one that had gone missing from my closet about six months previous. Her always colorful hair was now a shimmering ice blue. She wore it down so that it rested just at her shoulders and I could see hints of week-old waves. It was disheveled and gorgeous, with small strands of her side-swept bangs falling across her eye.

"Woah," was once again my opener.

A smile crept across her lips, just below glistening golden eyes.

"Hello, Alex," she said as a single tear rolled down her cheek.

Her voice was muffled as it passed through the thick glass.

"Hi," I managed.

We stared at each other for a few seconds before I finally spoke again.

"What are you doing here?" I asked.

"I used to work here, remember?"

"Yeah, I know, but what made you come in here?"

"They called it an 'airborne virus.' That sounds like the kind of thing that we would put people in here for. So I grabbed a bunch of food and my phone and came in here. In retrospect I should have grabbed a charger too."

I let out an involuntary chuckle at that last part. It was good to see that she hadn't changed. She was always more of a "ready, fire, aim" kind of girl.

"I guess you found one?"

"Yeah, somebody left one in a drawer in here behind some stuff. When my phone finally came on I had a voicemail from you. That's when I texted you."

"You got my voicemail and you texted me? Why didn't you call?"

She looked genuinely puzzled. "Why would I call when I could text?"

"Because it's the end of the world? Because a text is a little casual for the apocalypse?"

Her quizzical expression remained.

"Also that was hours ago," I continued.

"Yeah, I was driving myself crazy waiting for a response so I took a nap."

"You took a nap?"

"Yeah. And then I woke up and saw your response."

"And then you called me anyway. In response to the question I texted you."

"Oh yeah, it was way too much for a text."

I shook my head in frustration. "You know what, never mind. How much food do you have in there?"

She looked around the room at the various snacks and such, including a duffle bag which appeared to be mostly full.

"Um, maybe enough for a couple more weeks. Less if we can get you in here and we have to share. Maybe you should get some more food and bring it with you."

It would seem that neither of us had fully considered the hopeless reality of the situation until that moment.

"Charlie," I responded cautiously, "I…I can't come in there. I'm infected."

A look of panic crossed her face. "You're what?"

"Yeah, of course I am. Don't worry. It doesn't really affect me. But I'm still a carrier."

She said nothing, but instead took a small step back while keeping her gaze fixed on me. Her eyes darted back and forth, studying my face the way Shayra had when I had visited her in the hospital a few days before. She opened her mouth to speak but no words came out.

"Listen," I started softly, "we're going to figure this out. I saw a convenience store just down the road on the way here. I'm going to run get something to eat, and then I'm going to come right back and see if I can find a pillow and some blankets."

She nodded slowly, still scanning my face.

"I'm going to stay and sleep right here outside this door tonight, ok?"

She let out a deep sigh.

"Ok," she said finally.

When I returned from my errands a few minutes later, she had made herself a pallet just on the other side of the glass out of the linens available inside the quarantine room. After a quick dinner of potato chips and mini donuts, we settled into our beds. We lay in silence for several minutes before I noticed we were both pressing against the glass on our respective sides. It was the closest thing we could have to physical contact and we had both done it so naturally.

"Charlie?" I said as I rolled over on my side to face her.

She mirrored my movement and rolled to face me. I could barely see her eyes in the dim illumination from the security light down the hall.

"Yeah?" she answered.

"This wasn't Shayra's fault."

She smiled at me with a tired smile.

"I know it wasn't," she said.

23

Monday, April 26th, 2032

Sleeping on the hard floor of the hospital proved to be a less than ideal arrangement. I spent most of the night tossing and turning. Owed partially to my uncomfortable bed and the same recurring dream I had when I was upside-down in the Prius, but mainly caused by a dilemma that had been growing persistently in my mind since I arrived the previous day. I sat with my back to the white plastic frame of the quarantine room door with my left shoulder pressed up against the glass. I stared down the hallway, past the leaves and collecting places for dust, as I mulled it over.

It was a simple problem, really. Charlie was inside the quarantine room, safe from the nano-organisms. That was good. I was outside with the nano-organisms, but was mostly unaffected by them. That was also good. But these two good things together added up to a seemingly insurmountable bad thing. She was in there, and I was out here, and that was the only way she could stay safe.

Then there was the food issue. I had long been formulating a theory that once the human population had died off, the nano-organisms would follow soon after. With no host, they couldn't last long. But as for exactly how long, I had no way of knowing. And inside the quarantine room, Charlie had only enough food for a couple of weeks.

If I could find a way to get her more food, even enough to last until the nano-organisms had died out, I was still a carrier. She could never be truly safe from being infected as long as I was still around, which meant, most likely, I would have to—

"Good morning," came Charlie's soft voice from the other side of the glass.

I was more than thankful for the derailment of my increasingly dismal train of thought.

"I'm guessing you didn't sleep very well?" she inquired.

"Not really. You?"

"Not bad."

That wasn't really a surprise. Charlie had always been one of those people who could sleep pretty much anywhere at anytime. We had watched the first half of about thirty movies because she couldn't hang on until the end. After an exciting scene I would turn to see her reaction, only to find her asleep with her phone in her hand, usually with her finger still in the scrolling position. Shayra said she thought Charlie had undiagnosed narcolepsy. But I guessed that things like sitting still for two hours and staring at a screen were just too boring and ordinary for a girl like her.

She readjusted to a sitting position with her back also resting against the door frame and her right shoulder against the glass. It was the closest she could come to leaning on my shoulder.

"So what's the plan for today?" she asked.

I turned to face her. "What do you mean?"

"Well, I was so excited to see you yesterday, I didn't even think to ask what you're doing here. You're here for a reason, right?"

"I came to see you," I said with a smile.

"Nice try," she countered. "You didn't even know I was here until we talked yesterday."

"Yes, but your hair puts off a homing signal. I could spot it from hundreds of miles away."

"Spill it, Lee."

She always called me by my last name when she was done playing games.

I sighed. "Well, um, Shayra sent me here."

She sat up excitedly and looked right into my eyes.

"To save the world," I finished.

She stared at me for a moment in seeming disbelief before a childish looking grin swept across her face.

"Heck yes," she said with a nod. "When do we start?"

I leaned away from her abruptly.

"*We* don't," I said sharply.

"What? What is that supposed to mean?"

"That room is the only place you're safe. You have to stay in there until I can figure something out."

"Ooh, safety," she said sarcastically. "Sounds fun."

"Look, I'll figure something out. I promise."

She didn't respond. Instead she did a kind of smile with her lips pressed together. The kind you flash the guy at work you barely know when you pass him in the hall. I knew exactly what that smile meant. She had officially stopped listening. I pushed myself to standing.

"Ok, look, according to my phone there's a Target about five minutes from here. I'm going to go get some decent bedding for tonight, and when I get back we can figure it out. Sound good?"

She simply nodded, maintaining her hallway courtesy smile. Without another word, I turned and made my way down the hall towards the covered drive where I had left the Range Rover.

I didn't want to have this fight with her. I couldn't. Not when there were so many other things going on that demanded my full effort and attention. As I opened the vehicle door, I determined to put it out of my mind. If there was one thing I knew about Charlie, it was that she didn't take orders. At the end of the day, or usually much sooner, she would do exactly what she wanted to do.

I pulled back up to entrance C at AllianceHealth about thirty minutes later with a car load of pillows and blankets. I had probably ended up with considerably more than I actually needed, but I wanted to make sure I could create a comfortable sleeping experience for myself and, if I could figure out how to get it to her, for Charlie as well. As I did my best to get a sufficient grip on both the pillows and the comforters I had picked out, it dawned on me that, over the course of our relationship, we had never discussed whether or not she was allergic to down. I kicked myself for not grabbing a couple of hypoallergenic pillows, just to be safe.

I waddled down the hallway towards the quarantine wing with two pillows under each arm and a comforter in each hand.

"So, I hope you're not allergic to goose feathers," I said when I finally reached the line of glass windows. "Or is it duck feathers? I guess I don't actually know what down is made of. Anyway, I can always go back once we figured out how to get all this into the room with—"

I stopped in place about fifteen feet from the room where Charlie had been. As the sight before me registered in my mind, my grip involuntarily released and the bedding I had been carrying slid to the floor.

The door was open.

24

"Hello, Alex," came a voice from behind me.

I didn't want to turn around. I didn't want to believe what all the evidence was telling me. Her voice was no longer muffled. It was as clear as I had heard Patrick's the day before. The faint and familiar smell of dragon fruit wafted through the musty air, recalling more memories than I had the time or emotional capacity to sort through.

After gathering my courage, I turned slowly. She stood just a few feet away, dimly backlit by the security light down the hall. She reached up with her right hand and brushed the silver blue hair out of her face. A single tear rolled down her cheek as she mustered a sheepish smile.

For six months I had dreamed of running my hand through that hair. I had thought repeatedly about touching her hand or her cheek one more time. And yet in that moment I desperately wanted nothing more than for her to be untouchable. Alive and safe, behind the glass. But she wasn't. In fact, she had already started to die.

"Why?" I said horsely.

It was the only word that would come out of my mouth. The only question on my mind.

Why would she take away the last person I loved?

"What?" she said with a confused smile.

"Why would you do that? I told you..." I paused for a moment. I could feel the anger rising up and sharpening my tone. "I told you we would figure something out. Why could you not just trust me?"

She smiled compassionately.

"Alex…" She took a step towards me as she spoke.

When I recoiled, her smile disappeared.

"You were the last person in my life who was still safe," I continued, getting angrier as I spoke. "Why couldn't you just let me keep that?"

I felt myself losing control of my emotions, but I didn't care. She had gone too far this time. She had committed the ultimate act of selfishness.

"You just had to do it, didn't you?" I was yelling now. "You had to open that door and take the last thing I loved away!"

Her smile turned to a frown as she once again started moving towards me. This time I held my ground. She stopped when she was about a foot and a half from my face.

"I can't believe you would do that," I continued. "To be that selfish. To just be that—"

Her hand landed flat against my cheek with a clap before I even realized she had raised it. I recoiled once more, but this time in shock. I reached up and started rubbing my cheek in pain.

"What the crap?" I yelled.

Before I could step back any further, she advanced towards me until her face was inches from mine and her accusatory finger was nearly touching the tip of my nose.

"Let's get one thing straight right now, Alexander," she said through gritted teeth. "I have lived on my own terms and I will die on my own terms. No one else's. Do you understand me? If I want to spend the rest of my life, however short, out here with you instead of dying of hunger in a human display case, you better believe that's what I'm gonna do. Got it?"

After a few seconds, I indicated my agreement with a quick but subtle nod. She lowered her hand and allowed a mischievous smile to creep back onto her face.

"Good," she said. "Let's go."

With that, she turned and started towards the exit.

It took me a minute or two to get moving again after the roller-coaster of emotion I had just experienced, but I soon caught up with Charlie at the Range Rover. In silence, we climbed in to our respective seats and I pressed the ignition button.

"You know, we're going to have to talk about this at some point," I started hesitantly.

"There's nothing to talk about," she quipped as she reached over to grab her seatbelt. "I told you, my terms."

"Not that. We're going to have to talk about what happened between us. Six months ago."

Her head shot up. "What? Why?"

"Because otherwise we're in for a really tense couple of days until you—" I stopped myself and gave that sentence some more thought. "I…I just want to clear the air between us, that's all."

She was doing that smile again. The one with her lips pressed together.

"Fine," she said after a moment. "What about it?"

"Just what I said. What happened?"

"What do you mean what happened? You proved that you weren't ready to be married so I moved on."

"Was it really that easy? We were together for two years!"

She stared down at her lap and fiddled with the ring on her right hand.

"No, ok? It wasn't easy at all. It sucked. But what was I supposed to do?"

"I made a mistake, Charlie."

"No, Alex. It was bigger than that. I couldn't spend the rest of my life wondering every day if that would be the day you came home and told me you got fired again. And what if we had kids? Then there would be diapers and baby food to worry about. I just couldn't do it. You needed to grow up and I couldn't make you. So I thought—"

She stopped and looked out the window.

"You thought what?" I pressed.

She turned back and looked me straight in the eyes, her cheeks glistening in the morning sun from tears I hadn't seen fall.

"I thought that if I left it would finally be enough to make you grow up, but it wasn't. I left, and you stayed. So, I made myself move on."

She let out a sniffle and turned her face back towards her lap.

"Are you saying you broke up with me to try and trick me into coming after you?" I said, not really trying to hide my annoyance.

She closed her eyes and shook her head. "No. I broke up with you because I couldn't pretend that your irresponsibility wasn't a problem anymore. Because if I didn't walk away at that point, I never would have. I believed that you could be better, but when I left and you didn't even try, you proved that you didn't want to be."

I hung my head. I couldn't even argue because I knew she was right. I had let her down. In fact, I didn't seem to be capable of anything else. I had let my parents down when I didn't get married and give them grandchildren. I had let Shayra down when I triggered the replication of the nano-organisms. I had even let

Patrick down when I left him to die at the Deer Creek Lodge.

"I'm sorry," I said. "I don't know what to say."

When I finally looked over at her, the last thing I expected was to see her smiling. But that's exactly what I saw.

"But look at you, Alex," she chuckled. "Here you are. Off to save the world. Being exactly who I knew you could be all along."

I allowed the slightest grin to cross my lips as I shrugged. "Yeah, I guess."

She reached over and placed her hand on my knee and I felt my heart rate accelerating. It was the first time we had touched in over six months.

"Look," she said, "the past is in the past. We both made some mistakes but we're here now. So what's the plan?"

I looked at her quizzically as I reached towards my pocket. I had saved a copy of Shayra's letter to my phone and I decided that it could give a better explanation than I could.

"What mistakes did you make?" I asked.

She released her hold of my knee and settled back in her seat. "Well, none that I can think of. I was more just being polite."

I stared at her blankly to communicate that I was not amused by that comment, but she just smiled at me. That was her usual play when she said something that was just a little too honest. As much as I wanted to, I couldn't stay mad for long when she did that.

I navigated to Shayra's letter and handed Charlie my phone.

"Here," I said, "this explains most of it."

25

"Ok, so let's start with the museums in this area and work our way across town," Charlie said.

I had barely finished telling her what Patrick had said about how the cloning facility was possibly located in an old museum and she was already typing away on her phone. I would have attributed it to the fact that she knew she only had forty eight hours to live, but this was actually pretty typical behavior for her. She was always in the moment, leaping before she looked.

"One who insists on seeing with perfect clarity before they decide, never decides," she used to say.

As she waited for the page to load, I realized I was staring at her. Five minutes ago she was in my face telling me that she would live how she wanted, and now she was pouring everything into helping me. As I watched, she absentmindedly brushed her hair behind her ear to keep it from blocking her view. She looked serious but her beauty remained soft. She had cried off and wiped away most of her eye make up and yet her eyes were still captivating.

"Here," she said abruptly. "Oklahoma Museum of Flying. That's the closest one. It's near a small airport in Bethany."

"I'm sorry," I blurted out.

"What? Sorry for what?"

"Everything. Everything I put you through."

"Oh, forget about it. It's all past stuff."

"No. I mean yeah, it is, but I just want to say I get it. I get why you left. I get why you didn't want to marry me anymore."

She sighed heavily. "Alex, can we maybe not do this right now?"

"Oh. Yeah, sure."

She turned back to her phone and I let a moment or two pass.

"So, when do you want to talk about it?" I prodded.

She threw her head back against the headrest in frustration and closed her eyes. Without looking, she pointed her finger towards the windshield.

"Just drive," she said.

We pulled up to the Oklahoma Museum of Flying about ten minutes later. It was a small, prefabricated metal building hidden in the middle of a larger airport complex. Red plastic letters across the face of the building announced its name just above three windows and a glass door. A blue canvas awning covered the last six feet of the sidewalk that led to the main entrance. Before I had even put the vehicle in park, Charlie was already unbuckling.

"Let's get it," she said with a crooked grin before opening the door and climbing out.

If I didn't know any better, I would have thought she was enjoying this. She was excited, giddy even.

I hung my head again at that thought. The truth was that I didn't really know any better. We had dated for two years, and yet I had never truly gotten to know her. At least, not in any way that really mattered. Not any more than was necessary to avoid causing a fight.

"You coming?" Her voice came from just outside the Range Rover's open tailgate.

She already had the tire iron in her hand and was heading for the glass door before the tailgate even finished closing. She used it to smash through the glass without skipping a beat. She turned back towards me and smiled again as I climbed out of the driver seat.

"I've always wanted to break in somewhere without going to jail," she chuckled.

"Have you broken in somewhere *with* going to jail before?" I asked reluctantly.

She hesitated for a moment. "Uh, yeah, juvie. I thought I told you that."

"Yeah," I lamented, "you probably did."

We stepped through the broken glass door and into the open expanse of the building. After locating the light switch a few feet down the wall from the front door, we were able to see that most of the museum was one large room. There were various pieces of vintage equipment and flight paraphernalia scattered around the perimeter, some in and some out of glass display cases, as well as several small airplanes in different states of restoration. A particularly well kept plane in the corner was adorned in red, white, and blue paint with the words "*Miss America*" across the side in script lettering.

"So what happened?" I asked.

"What?" Charlie answered, barely paying attention.

"How did you end up in juvie?"

"I, uh, broke into a Starbucks."

"What? Why?"

She turned away from the displays and looked me straight in the eye. "I wanted coffee."

I had to chuckle at that one.

"Wow. I don't guess I've ever wanted coffee that much."

She turned back towards the displays.

"Yeah, well, the heart wants what it wants," she said flippantly. "Anyway, I probably wouldn't have ended up in jail if it wasn't for the thing with the judge."

"Oh, this I've got to hear."

"When I went before the judge, he asked me if I really thought that getting a cup of coffee was worth breaking the law."

"And?"

"I said 'Obviously.' So he sentenced me to three months. He said I needed to learn a lesson."

"And did you?" I asked with a playful smile.

“Yeah, I learned that there’s a twenty-four hour coffee shop two blocks away from the one I broke into.”

I couldn’t help but break into laughter at that comment.

“Shut up! I was fifteen!” she said indignantly as she turned and slapped me across the arm.

“Dang. Where were your parents during all of this?”

That was a mistake. As soon as I said it, I remembered. Her smile dissolved and her face got serious.

“Um, my dad had already moved out and my mom was still in the psych ward,” she said flatly.

“Charlie, I’m sorry. I knew that and I just… forgot. I didn’t mean to—”

“It’s fine, Alex,” she interrupted. “Let’s just forget it.”

We stood in awkward silence for a moment, distracting ourselves from the tension by glancing around at the different exhibits. Finally, she raised an arm and pointed at what appeared to be offices, taking up the bottom half of the room along the north wall.

“Maybe there’s something in there,” she said.

She started towards one of the wooden doors and I trailed a few feet behind her. I decided it might be worth it to try and lighten the mood.

"I guess it's good you didn't want to marry me. Sounds like it would have been up to me to bail you out of jail the next time you wanted coffee."

She stopped and turned to face me. Her serious expression from my previous comment remained.

"Why do you keep saying it like that?" she snapped.

"Like what?" I asked, genuinely confused.

She narrowed her eyes at me. "You keep saying that I didn't want to marry you."

"But you didn't. I got fired and you decided you didn't want to marry me anymore. Right?"

"No. That's not right at all. It wasn't about what I wanted or didn't want."

"Charlie, I've never known you to do anything you didn't want to do. Or more specifically, I've never known you to *not* do something that you did want to do."

She reached up and started rubbing her forehead in frustration. "Just so I know, how many more times are we going to have to have this conversation?"

I didn't answer her question, but rather continued waiting for her to answer mine. She closed her eyes and let out a sigh.

"Look, like I just said, it wasn't about that," she explained. "I had to walk away in order to protect myself. Because I couldn't live in that kind of uncertainty. But I never—"

She stopped and squeezed her lips together, as if she was trying to prevent herself from finishing that sentence.

"Never what?" I pressed.

She sighed again. "I never stopped wanting to marry you."

"Oh. I guess I didn't realize—Wait, *never*?"

"Come on, Lee," she snapped. "We're burning daylight."

With that, she spun on the ball of her foot and marched towards the wooden door at the back of the room, not really concerning herself with whether or not I'd be joining her.

26

By the time we finished at the Oklahoma Museum of Flying it was nearing midday. As we drove to our next stop, Charlie was going through the list of museums in the city, trying to determine which ones would be worth checking for the cloning facility.

"The Museum of Art is just one of the museums in that part of town. It looks like there's five total. There's a telephone history museum, a banjo museum, a memorial to the—"

"Wait," I interrupted, "did you say a banjo museum?"

She looked a little closer at her phone screen. "Yeah, that's what it says. Banjo history and memorabilia."

"You've got to be kidding."

"Oh, that's not even the weirdest one on the list. Wait until we get to the American Pigeon Museum."

"Ok, now you're just making stuff up," I laughed.

She smiled back at me. "Oklahoma, bro."

"Wow. Ok, so what about this next one?"

She tapped away at her phone for a few seconds, I assumed calling up their website.

"The Museum of Art is way bigger than the flying one. It's three stories and it's connected to some sort of visual arts center. This one will probably take awhile to get through."

We had just taken the I-40 exit off of I-44 when I noticed that the needle on the Range Rovers gas gauge was dangerously near empty.

"Uh oh." I pointed towards the gauge.

She looked up from her phone. "What's wrong?"

"We're almost out of gas."

"Ok," she said after a few more taps, "take the Western exit like the directions say, but instead of turning on 5th, go down to Reno. We'll pass right by a gas station on our way to the museum."

I looked at her as she spoke, but I couldn't help linger for a few extra seconds once she was done. She had walked away from safety to be here for me. She had given up the rest of her life to help me for two days. I didn't deserve that kind of devotion. I couldn't even process it. I had never in my life been that selfless. She was the most amazing woman on the planet, and if I had just fastened that safety harness back at Lockheed Martin then I would be able to call this amazing woman my wife.

I turned my eyes back to the road as a new thought hit me. If we had gotten married and stayed in Fort Worth, she would have died the same day as Shayra. The same day as Shelly, the security guard, and Nurse Kristen.

I mindlessly watched the white stripes on the highway pass beneath the tires of the Range Rover. By this point, I had gotten used to being the only vehicle on the road.

So many things that I had only seen in movies and video games had now become common place. There was nothing left of my old way of life. Amidst that reality, it seemed almost ridiculous to consider what might have been if it hadn't been for a safety violation. If Charlie had still been in Fort Worth she would be dead and I would be doing this alone. But I wasn't. She was with me, and she was pouring the remainder of her life into helping me. And here, at the end of everything, I couldn't ask for anything more.

The sign announcing the Western Avenue exit caught my attention. I signaled out of habit and moved over to the exit lane. Charlie snickered at my use of the blinker before she turned to look out over the empty city. As she did, her smile all but faded. It seemed that the irony of my signal usage started a new train of thought in her head. I'd had some time to adjust to these new realities, but she hadn't. Up until a few hours ago, she had been sheltered from all of this.

"It's so quiet," she observed. "I always kind of thought that the end of the world would be way more violent and noisy. But it's just…empty. Like going out on Christmas day when all the stores are closed."

"Yeah," I responded casually, "you get used to it."

She turned back towards me.

"Do you?" she asked somberly.

"Well, no. Not really. But you learn not to think about it too hard, I guess."

She smiled again just a little as she turned and looked back out the window. By now, we had reached the gas station on Reno. I pulled up at a random pump and pressed the ignition button to shut off the engine. As I reached for the handle to exit the vehicle, Charlie's voice stopped me.

"Were you there when she died?" she asked abruptly.

I stopped, but I couldn't look back at her. Instead, I let my gaze rest on the door handle. I took a deep breath as I tried to stop all the memories from rushing back. Yet despite that effort, I could almost hear the doctor yelling to Nurse Kristen in my head.

Squeal. Pop. Thud.

"Yeah," I answered simply, "I was."

"Good," she nodded. "That's good. Dying alone is just about the worst thing I can think of."

"Watching the ones that you care about die and having to just keep living isn't all that great either."

She sat up straight in her chair, a look of uncertainty on her face. I had to admit the cynicism of that statement surprised even me.

"Alex, promise me something," she said, all but ignoring my comment. "When it's my time, don't be sad."

I couldn't help but chuckle a bit. "Don't be sad? Like it's just that easy?"

"I mean it. It won't help anything. You've got a job to do and you don't need to waste time on crap like that. This was my choice and I don't regret it even a little bit, ok? Don't be sad. Just make it count for something and finish this. Promise me."

I didn't answer right away. How could I promise something like that? Why would she even ask me to?

"Alex!" she said impatiently.

"Yes, ok," I conceded. "I will try my best."

She settled back into her chair with a sigh. "Good."

I climbed out of the front seat and made my way back to the gas pump. I pulled up Shayra's credit card on my phone and tapped it against the RF icon next to the keypad. A beep indicated the card was approved and the screen prompted me to select a fuel grade. It didn't seem to matter what I picked, so I went with premium. As the numbers started rising on the digital readout, I passed the time by casually scanning the street. There were several taller buildings off to the north-east. The tallest of them had a faintly visible flashing red light on the top, indicating its height for any low flying airplanes. I guessed that part of town was where we would find the Museum of Art.

I shifted my attention to the immediate area. The gas station sat on the south-east corner of the intersection of Reno and Classen. I watched as the traffic lights in the intersection changed from green to yellow, then to red, and then back again.

But then, as I watched, all the lights in the intersection went black. I squinted my eyes to make sure it wasn't a trick of the harsh noon sunlight, but it made no difference. Suddenly, the realization hit me that I no longer heard the gas flowing behind me. I turned to see that the LCD on the pump had also gone blank.

A power outage? Maybe a blown transformer?

I looked off to the north-east where I had seen the light on top of the building. I waited, hoping for a faint red flash in the distance, but it never came. As much as I wanted to think that it was merely a problem at a local substation, I knew the truth. With all the power plants abandoned, and no workers there to maintain them, the entire Oklahoma City power grid had gone down.

27

"So what now?" Charlie asked, sounding way calmer than I felt.

"I don't know." I was checking my phone to see if the internet was still working. "Looks like cell towers went down with the power."

"Ok, so what did people do before the internet?"

"Not know who actually won arguments?" I tried to lighten the mood.

She was in full problem solving mode and did not find my joke amusing. Of course, that was not specific to her problem solving mode.

"I mean when they wanted to find a specific place, genius," she responded sharply.

I thought for a moment.

"I don't know. When I was a kid, I remember my parents looking places up in the phone book."

"They haven't printed those in years. Oh, what about those pamphlets?"

"What?"

"You remember pamphlets! At hotels and museums they always have that rack with little leaflets about other local attractions. Maybe they'll have some at the art museum."

"Yes!" I recalled. "I saw some of those at the Deer Creek Lodge!"

The gas tank on the Range Rover had reached less than a quarter of a tank full before the pump had shut down. I moved the gear selector into the drive position and started the vehicle moving in the direction of the art museum, hoping it would be enough.

"I used to love Frontier City," Charlie reminisced as we perused the rack of pamphlets.

The Museum of Art gave us little trouble gaining entry to the building thanks to the glass doors at the main entrance. The building was mostly dark except for a few select security lights that were seemingly running on some kind of emergency back up power. I took a guess that the rest of the security system was probably also running on backup power. I assumed that a silent alarm had been triggered and a very obvious red light was flashing on a console at an empty police dispatch station somewhere nearby. At least that's what always seemed to happen in the movies.

We made a stop at the gift shop to grab a printed map of the city and as many OKCMOA mini flashlights as we could fit in our pockets before returning to the pamphlet rack near the main entrance. Charlie, staying true to her nature, was getting distracted by the most colorful pamphlets.

"They have this ride called the Brain Drain and it takes you in a loop and then stops at the top so you're just hanging there upside down. It's insane!"

"I don't think that's what we're looking for."

"Oh yeah," she turned to me with a smile. "Pigeon museum, right?"

I sighed and shook my head but I couldn't help but crack a smile. Charlie knew exactly how to keep the mood light, even under the worst circumstances. Now, having her here, I couldn't imagine if I had to do this on my own. And yet, in less than forty-eight hours—

"You know," I said as I pushed the thought down, "I think just grab any pamphlet that says anything about a museum and we'll sort through them later in the car."

After looking through the entire selection, we gathered about twenty pamphlets referencing some kind of museum. I tucked them away in my back pocket and we made our way down the hallway towards the exhibits.

We spent the better part of three hours searching the three public floors of the museum, the attached performing arts center, and the cafe at the far east end of the building. The only part of the building we had not searched was the back rooms and corridors meant only for staff. The doors that would give us access to this area were all discrete and colored to match the wall into which they were barely recessed. They were also secured with an RF receiver for entry using employee badges, much like the Lykos facility at Western Place.

The heavy security door provided a bit of an entry problem, but Charlie quickly solved it with the bottom end of a nearby metal stanchion. Between my suggested point of impact based on recent experience with doors and her two years competing in the Fort Worth city softball league, it only took two hits before we were gazing down the blank white hallway behind the door. Neither of us started down the hallway immediately and I could tell we were thinking the same thing. The hallway looked sterile, like a hospital, and the fluorescent security lights every twenty-five feet or so gave it an eerie green cast.

As I expected, Charlie was the first one to step forward into the hall. I followed close behind her, retrieving two of the mini flashlights from my pocket and handing one to her.

"We probably need to see if we can find some badges so we don't have to carry this stand thing around with us," she whispered.

"Look," I said, directing the beam of my flashlight towards a sign on the first door inside the hallway.

"Security," she read it out loud. "Boom."

The stanchion was a little more difficult to maneuver in the narrow hallway so it took a few extra hits to gain us entry. Once inside, we found the room ironically devoid of security lights, leaving it completely dark. We used our flashlights to scan the walls for anywhere it looked like they might store extra badges. A small, grey metal lockbox on the wall to the left seemed like the most likely place.

Without a word, Charlie switched off her flashlight and tucked it into her pocket before lifting a nightwatchman's baton from a hook on the nearby wall. I instinctively turned my face away as she raised it in the air and stepped towards the lockbox. The resonant crashing sound echoed out the door and down the sterile hallway, causing me to cover my ears.

After two more crashes, I heard the muffled sound of the baton hitting the concrete below our feet. I turned to see the door of the lockbox laying twisted on the floor and Charlie standing next to it with a white rectangular badge in her hand. She retrieved the flashlight from her pocket and started towards the door.

"You coming?" she said as she passed me briskly.

28

Charlie was not like most girls. Apart from her obviously unique sense of style, she didn't handle her emotions the way they did. She was a textbook internalizer. While most girls I had known, my sister included, liked to talk through it when they were upset, Charlie would simply get quiet. The only way you could detect that something was on her mind was through changes in behavior, such as aggression towards inanimate objects. After seeing the way she destroyed that lockbox, I had begun to suspect that something was on her mind.

For fifteen minutes or so we explored the staff area of the OKC Museum of Art, mostly in silence. Every so often we would find another room to check, and after finding nothing of interest, she would let out a "Huh," and we would move on to the next area.

Finally, her vocabulary opened up a bit when we came across a break room illuminated by a single florescent light, complete with fully stocked vending machines and a fridge full of soft drinks.

"Aw, heck yes," she muttered.

Stress eating was another sign that she was upset. She picked up one of the folding chairs in the room and used it to smash the glass on the front of one of the machines. I shielded my eyes out of reflex as shards of broken glass flew in every direction. Having accomplished her goal, she tossed the chair aside.

"Charlie," I started cautiously, "is something on your mind?"

"Yeah," she answered without breaking her gaze away from the vending machine, "barbecue potato chips."

She reached passed the broken glass and grabbed three bags.

"Charlie," I said, this time a little sterner.

She turned around to face me. She was pressing her lips together again.

“It’s nothing,” she said finally. “Seriously.”

I motioned towards one of several fold-up card tables in the room. She threw her head back and sighed.

“I don’t want to talk about it, Alex. Why do you always try and make me talk about it?”

“Because you’re upset. And I want to help you not be upset. I’m trying to be a good…whatever I am. Friend, I guess.”

A flash of sadness crossed her face at the word friend, and then quickly changed to uncertainty. We stood at an impasse for a long moment, her clutching her chips and me with my arm outstretched towards the nearest table.

“Fine,” she said as she stormed over and dropped the chips on the table.

We stared at each other for another minute or two without speaking. I knew better than to try and coax anything out of her. I was lucky enough that she agreed to come sit down. I was going to have to let her tell me what was bothering her on her own terms. She sat quietly for a moment before looking up at me. She was trying to maintain a strong, controlled expression, but eyes that glistened in the dim glow of the loan security light betrayed her.

"They're gone," she tried to smile, but her voice was thick with emotion. "Everyone I've ever known is gone."

I should have known this moment was coming. But Charlie was always so strong, I never could have fully prepared myself for seeing her look this broken. I could tell she had been holding this in for a while. When she finally admitted what was bothering her, she looked utterly defeated. My heart broke for her. Mainly because I knew exactly what she was going through, but also because the only one left to comfort her was me. And I was all but useless at that sort of thing.

I mustered as much compassion as I could, "Yeah, I know."

"My aunt, my coworkers, my best friend Kate. Just like that."

I said nothing, but instead held her gaze.

"I'm sorry." She sat back in her chair. "It's just all kind of hitting me. You've probably already been through this."

"Yeah, I have."

"How did you get past it? You seem fine now."

"It comes and goes. I have moments when I'm fine and then the next moment I'm not. I guess I just try not to dwell on it too much, you know? Focus on the task at hand and all that."

"Yeah, I guess that makes sense."

She sat in silence for a few seconds and stared thoughtfully out into the hall. I could tell she wanted to say more, but she was still processing it.

"I just always thought I would have another chance, you know?" she said finally.

I cocked my head inquisitively. "Another chance for what?"

"To fix things. Broken relationships, stuff like that."

Getting her to open up about her feelings was a little like a scavenger hunt. You had to follow the little clues to try and get to the destination. She clearly wasn't talking about me, because a relationship do-over was exactly what we had been offered. She wasn't talking about her mom because she had passed away a year or so before we met. I went for the only other logical choice.

"You mean your dad?" I tried.

She looked down at the table and I could see her physically holding back a full meltdown. After collecting herself for a second she looked back towards me.

A tear rolled down each of her cheeks as the words came softly. "The last time I talked to him was over a year ago. I told him that I didn't ever want to see him again."

"I remember that."

"I told him that he had walked out on me and mom and I could never forgive him for that. But in the back of my mind I always thought that if I ever wanted to forgive him, he'd be there. Just waiting for me to be ready."

She couldn't hold it in anymore. Her face contorted as a sob broke through.

"But he won't," she said through the tears. "They're all gone and I missed my chance. I'll never get that back."

There was nothing more I could say. I stood from my chair and moved to a kneeling position next to hers. I reached my arms around her and pulled her close, letting the side of her face rest on my shoulder. For several minutes neither of us spoke. I simply let her cry until the tears subsided. After I felt like enough time had passed, I slowly pulled back from her and brought my hands to rest on hers.

"We can only start from here," I whispered.

She smiled just enough to tell me she recognized the words from Shayra's letter.

"Tomorrow is a new day," she quoted the next line.

I reached up and ran my fingers across her cheek, clearing away the trail of a tear. “That’s my girl.”

I stood, ready to continue our search, but she gripped my hands tightly.

“There’s something else,” she said with a sniffle. “Something I’ve been thinking about since I read Shayra’s letter.”

“Oh, ok. What’s up?”

“You said the nano things or whatever don’t really hurt you, but you’re still a carrier, right?”

“Yeah. I mean, that’s what I got from the letter.”

“And the plan is to basically find this cloning facility, cook up a new batch of humans, and hang out to keep an eye on everything until they pop?”

“Pretty much.”

“Ok. So assuming you do all that, and all the nano guys in the air have died out in nine months or how ever long it takes to grow these clones. What about you?”

I knew exactly where she was going with this. I had gone through this same conversation with myself.

“What about me?”

“If you’re a carrier, won’t all the clones get infected as soon as they’re born? You’ll be right back where you started, with everybody except you dead in a couple of days."

"Uh, yeah, maybe," I lied. "I haven't really thought about it that much."

"But Alex, what are you—"

"Hey," I interrupted, "I'm just taking everything one step at a time. There's no need to worry about any of that right now. Right now we just need to find the place."

She didn't look convinced.

"Yeah, I guess," she said hesitantly.

I held my hand out to help her up from her chair and she took it reluctantly. As we reached for our flashlights and turned back towards the dark hallway, she grabbed two bags of barbecue potato chips for the trip. I smiled at her as she walked past me to take the lead. But as she passed me, I let the forced smile fade away.

She was right. I had known for a while now. I wasn't sure how I was going to see this plan through or how I was going to take care of the clones once they were born. But the more I thought about it, the more I knew one thing for certain: In order for the human race to live on, I was going to have to die.

29

We spent the rest of the afternoon and evening searching the museums that remained in the area, a process made considerably slower with no electricity and no internet. We started with the northern most facility in the area, which was the OKC National Memorial, a museum dedicated the victims of the bombing that happened back in the nineteen nineties. From there, we worked our way south through the other three in the area. We ended at the American Banjo Museum on Sheridan. It was a two story salmon colored building that occupied the corner spot of a strip of connected buildings that, apart from the museum, was mostly restaurants.

We sat in the parking lot across the street planning our next move. It was well after 8:00 p.m. and the sun would have set before we could reach our next destination, leaving us without the helpful window light we had come to rely on in our searching. After some discussion, we settled on the idea of finding a place to rest for the night.

"Thompson's Woodland is a pretty nice neighborhood. It's just off of 44." Charlie had the map unfolded and was turning it this way and that. "If you take the 44 exit off of 235 and then exit Lincoln I think I can get us there. There's bound to be a house there that will work. That area is right in the middle of the other museums in the main part of the city. We can get back at it first thing in the morning and hit the Sports Hall of Fame on our way down to the History Center. That's a pretty big one. Eighteen acres, according to the brochure."

As she turned to me for confirmation of her plan I realized I was staring at her again and grinning like an idiot.

"What?" She sat up straight and brushed the hair out of her face.

My reflexes told me to look away but I ignored them and held her gaze for just another moment. Her eyes were striking. After her pink and yellow hair, it was the first thing I noticed about her the day we met. They were a grey blue color, piercing but soft, that almost matched her current hair color. They looked like a nebula in a far off galaxy but at the same time felt like finally getting home after a long and exhausting day.

"I've just missed you," I said finally, allowing my grin to grow slightly.

She smiled back at me. Even the ever dimming sunlight, spilling in though the Range Rover's windows, betrayed a slight glistening in her eyes.

"I've missed you, too."

She turned her head back towards the map, but her hand reached across the seat to take hold of mine.

Thompson's Woodland was a quiet area where all the houses had plenty of land so they weren't too close together. It reminded me of some of the neighborhoods you would find a few miles outside midsize Texas towns like Amarillo and Wichita Falls. The street was narrow with no sidewalk and barely room for two cars traveling opposite directions to pass safely without one of them having to veer off of the asphalt.

After we had passed five or six houses, I pulled off of the road and into a grassy area in front of them. I quickly switched off the Range Rover's engine to conserve what little gas we had left in the tank.

"Alright," I started as we climbed out of our respective doors and met at the front of the vehicle, "We need to figure out which one of these houses would work best. Something with a big living room so we can camp out in there. I know you won't want to share a bed, so that way we can be in the same room but nobody has to sleep on the floor. If we're lucky, we can find one with some clothes that will fit us both so we can change into clean clothes. Let's see if we can find one with a generator too so we have electricity. And maybe we can try and find one that looks like they're on vacation or something so we don't have to deal with week old dead bodies. So look and see if you see any empty mailboxes like their mail is being held or—"

"This one." Charlie's voice came from at least thirty yards away.

I turned to see her standing on the AC unit of the house behind me, peering over the fence into the back yard. She whipped her head back towards me, causing her hair to fly outward in a perfect shampoo commercial swish.

"It has a pool," she said as the hair settled, covering her right eye and accentuating her mischievous smile.

I tried to make my annoyance clear by the blank expression I held. "Seriously? Did you not hear what I was—"

She rolled her eyes at me. "And a generator."

That stopped me. "Oh. Really?"

She placed both hands on her hip and shifted her weight till it was resting smugly on one leg.

"And they're out of town," she continued, the smugness from her stance saturating her voice as well.

"Ok, how could you possibly know that?"

Without looking back she pointed to a small metal rectangle attached to the wood fence. "Beware of dog sign. No dog in the backyard. There's a food and water bowl back there, meaning the dog normally stays outside. But they've both been cleaned out, hence it's been boarded somewhere because they are out of town."

I couldn't tell her in that moment, but I was actually quite impressed that she had deduced all of that so quickly and easily. I probably shouldn't have been as surprised as I was. She was always brilliant.

I said nothing but rather hung my head in defeat and started towards the house. She hopped down from her perch atop the AC unit and met me at the front door.

"What now?" I asked. "Should I try and break it down?"

"Don't be such an animal," she said, her attitude from before still holding. She began scanning the porch area as she thought out loud. "They're out of town right? Surely they had somebody checking in on their house. Bringing in the mail, watering plants, stuff like that. Probably a neighbor. But if they had one person who could have checked in on things consistently, they could have just given them a copy of the key and left the dog for them to check in on regularly. But they didn't or they wouldn't have boarded it. Also there is mail in the mailbox, but not a lot so somebody has probably been taking it inside. Maybe different people. Meaning they probably had to hide a key somewhere on the…"

Before she finished her thought, she picked up a small turtle statue that sat conspicuously in the flower bed next to the porch and turned it over, revealing a small compartment containing a single key.

"Boom," she said at the discovery.

Now she was just showing off. She removed the key and unlocked the door, swinging it open with an over-the-top gesture.

"After you," she said sarcastically, holding her arm out in the direction of the entryway.

"Alright, calm down, Sherlock," I quipped as I walked past her and into the house.

Inside, we split up. I went for the living room and Charlie went in search of the kitchen.

The living room was large like I had hoped. The overstuffed couch and love seat I found there would be perfect for a good night's sleep. Opposite the seating was a large television mounted to the wall above a good sized fireplace. Between the two, several framed photos adorned a wooden mantel. The lives of the family that had lived here lined out in frozen moments. As I scanned the photos, a particular figure in one of them caught my eye. I moved closer to confirm what my eyes were telling me. Though in the photo her hair was a cotton candy pink, Charlie's face was unmistakable. She stood smiling between an overweight, balding man and a slender woman with curly hair outside the gates of Frontier City.

"Charlie?" I called to the other room.

"Yeah?" Her voice was muffled.

She entered the room with a chocolate sandwich cookie in her mouth and the rest of the package in her hand.

"Why is there a picture of you in these people's living room?" I asked, motioning towards the photograph.

Her eyes widened and she swallowed the food in her mouth.

"Awe, dang it!" She looked at me like a kid who had just been caught in a lie and she giggled. "Alright fine. This is my aunt and uncle's house. They told me they were going on a European cruise and I could stay here while they were gone."

In a way, the joke was almost more impressive than if her deductions had all been true. She made up those explanations in the moment and executed the con without a hint of deception.

"But I had you going with all that Sherlock stuff, didn't I?" she said as she poked me in the chest.

Although I'm nearly certain a hint of amusement broke through, I did my best to maintain an annoyed stare. Her smile dropped, but then it slowly returned as she sheepishly hunched her shoulders and let her head sink down into them. She pushed the package that was in her hand towards my direction.

"Cookie?" she offered.

30

Within half an hour we managed to get the generator running and had set up camp in the living room. Charlie had offered to take the love seat and let me have the roomier couch. I, of course, foolishly counter offered that she should take the couch. She graciously accepted.

Charlie had managed to find some jeans and a plain black t-shirt in her aunt's clothes. She was not as slender as her aunt, but as an older woman she bought her clothes a little looser. So when Charlie wore them they fit exactly the way she liked them.

I was not as lucky with her uncle's clothes. They were considerably beyond my size, so I had settled for a t-shirt and the smallest pair of sweatpants he owned while my clothes were in the washing machine.

We had decided we would shut the generator off through the night to conserve on fuel and so I was building up a solid arrangement of wood in the fireplace. I started with smaller twigs on the bottom and then leaned larger sticks against each other to form a sort of tent of firewood around the twigs.

"Did your dad show you how to do that?" Charlie asked me from the couch.

Once we got the generator going, her first priority was to immediately brew a pot of coffee. She had found a soft throw blanket in which to wrap herself, legs and all, and was sipping slowly out of a white mug that she held close with both hands. A typographical design painted in black across the side read "*Every little thing is going to be alright.*" I had chuckled at the irony when I had first seen it.

"Yeah, he used to tell me that using a fire starter was lazy." The memory made me smile. "He would tell me 'If you ever get stranded in the middle of nowhere there won't be any fire starters.'"

I looked over at the empty basket on the tile floor next to where the fireplace screen had been. I could tell by the smell inside the basket that it had contained paraffin fire starter blocks at one point.

"I guess he wasn't exactly wrong," I added.

"Do you think about them much?" she asked compassionately.

"Yeah. Well, kind of. I can't really let myself think about any of it too much."

"That makes sense. How did they handle the news about Shayra?"

I hesitated for only a moment. "I'm pretty sure they never found out."

"What? They must have said her name a million times between all the reports. How did they miss that?"

"They were at the cabin in Ruidoso. My dad called and asked how we were doing. I just couldn't—"

My voice faltered.

"You couldn't tell him that his baby girl had died," she finished for me.

I took a moment to collect myself.

"Losing my sister was the most painful thing I have ever felt," I said finally. "I would do anything to go back to a world where she was ok. My parents still had that. I just couldn't make myself take it away from them."

She smiled softly at me. "I think that's beautiful."

I sighed heavily. "It didn't feel that way."

She let the conversation sit for a few moments while she watched me ignite the firewood I had arranged. After a minute or two, I placed the screen back in front of the fire that was now roaring and made my way to the light switch to dim the over head light.

"I didn't get to say goodbye to anyone either." She spoke just above a whisper as she stared blankly into the flames, running her index finger up and down the side of her coffee mug.

Instead of settling into my place on the love seat, I sat on the couch next to her, my leg pressed up against hers. I rested my hand gently on her knee. She placed her hand on top of mine but continued staring into the fire.

"When my phone finally turned on, I had missed calls from my aunt and Kate. I still haven't been able to bring myself to listen to their voicemails."

"I thought I would never see you again," I blurted.

Her head twisted abruptly in my direction. I knew I had caught her off guard and possibly even upset her that I hadn't acknowledged her laments, but since I had gotten her first text, this second chance we'd been given had been nearly all I could think about.

"I'm sorry," I tried by best to recover. "I just—so much bad has happened. I wasn't there when my parents died. I didn't even get to bury my sister. The human race is collapsing but…you're here."

A smile slowly crossed her face and I saw her eyes start to glisten in the firelight.

"In my mind you were already dead," I continued. "I had already started trying to come to terms with it."

"And had you?" she asked.

"No," I answered quickly, not really needing to think about it. "I couldn't wrap my head around it. The idea that I had really lost you. I owed it to my sister to keep going, to see this plan through but, at times, even that was hard to believe in. It just all seemed so hopeless."

She nodded in understanding. I tried my best to blink back the tears forming in my eyes but I wasn't entirely successful.

"Then I got your text," I said as a single tear rolled down my cheek, "and it was like suddenly there was hope in the world again. Because you were still alive, the whole world was worth saving."

Without saying a word, she reached up and placed her hand on my cheek. Using her thumb, she wiped away the trail that the tear had left. She leaned in and pressed her lips against mine. I was so surprised by it that I almost forgot to kiss her back, but after the briefest moment, we both settled into it.

I don't know if it was because it was the end of the world, or if it was because I had been wanting to kiss her again since we broke up six months prior, but it seemed to me in that moment that it was the greatest kiss we had ever shared.

After a long moment, she finally pulled away. We looked into each others eyes for a second and then, without explanation, she stood to her feet. While maintaining eye contact, she grabbed the hem of her shirt and began to pull it upward. Immediately I grabbed her hands and stopped them in place.

"Charlie, no. What are you doing?"

"What am I doing?" she repeated with a chuckle. "Poor thing, did you opt out of that class in high school?"

I climbed frantically off of the couch and walked four or five steps away from her. "No, I know what you are doing I just mean—It can't happen like this. Or at all."

She released her hold on her shirt and her hands relaxed at her sides. "What? What are you talking about?"

"When we were engaged you said you wanted to wait until we were married to—to do that. And that's what I wanted too."

"Alex..."

"I just can't let you do it. I can't let the biggest physical thing to ever happen in our relationship be a regret for you. If we could get married and do this the right way then that would be different but we can't. And if we can't do it the right way, then I just can't let it happen at all."

I braced myself for her anger but was surprised when she quietly settled back into her seat on the couch.

"Yeah," she whispered. "Of course, you're right. That would have probably been a mistake."

I was doing my best not to make eye contact so as to keep my self control intact. "I'm going to run to the store, um, for a second and see if I can find some real food since all that's in the kitchen are snacks and stuff."

When I finally dared to look at her face, she was smiling sheepishly.

"Yeah, sounds good," she said.

I decided the best way to find a grocery store without a smart phone was to head back to the highway and drive until I saw something that fit the bill.

Thankfully I did, less then two miles away just off of the Classen exit. In just over an hour, I was turning back onto Willard loaded up with precooked bacon, german sausage, fresh vegetables, and various other items I had deemed still edible since the store lost electricity earlier that day.

As I entered the house, a panic began to creep up. The house was quiet and dark, except for the firelight coming from the living room. However, I could see from the entryway that there was far more light than should be coming from a fire the size of the one that I had built. I closed the front door, dropped the grocery bags and darted to the living room.

When I walked in I saw, not an out of control fire like I expected, but candles. The room was filled with them. I estimated at least forty. And standing in the center of the room wearing a black sleeveless dress with shoulders made of lace, was Charlie. The firelight danced off of her hair making it appear as orange and blue flames, cascading across the lace shoulders of her dress. At the sight, I took a moment to find my speech.

"Charlie, what's going on?" I said finally.

She smiled at me knowingly.

"You're right," she said softly. "If we're going to do this, we're going to do it right."

Before I realized what was happening, she was lowering herself down to one knee.

"Alexander Lee," she said, "will you marry me?"

31

I was suddenly very aware that I was wearing another man's baggy sweatpants. However, by the look on Charlie's face you never would have known it. She reached out to take my hand as I stepped closer.

"Well," she pressed, "what do you think? Will you do me the honor?"

"How?" I answered her question with one of my own. "Who will perform the ceremony?"

"We will."

"Does that count?"

She smiled from ear to ear and then let out a laugh, "Under the circumstances, I think God will be ok with it."

"Yeah, I guess. But—"

"I asked you a question," she interrupted. "Will you or won't you?"

"Charlie..."

"Will you or won't you?"

"Of course I will!" I snapped.

She flinched at my sudden answer. I softened my tone before continuing.

"Of course I will. It's all I've wanted since the first time I saw you."

I stepped towards her and reached for her hand. With a smile she took hold of mine and stood to her feet.

"So, what now?" I asked.

"Um, I don't know," she answered with a chuckle. "I'm kind of making this up as I go. I guess we should start with vows."

"I, uh, don't have anything prepared."

"Me neither. But maybe that will be better."

We joined both hands and she closed her eyes and took a deep, purposeful breath before looking into my eyes.

"Alex," she started, "I've never been good at talking about my feelings. Even when we were engaged. You know, the first time. But I think it's because I don't really feel much. At least not feelings for other people. I kind of do what I want and I don't really worry about how other people feel. But with you, that was always different. I couldn't really stop myself from caring about you. Or what you wanted. Or how you felt. But what's more, I didn't want to not care anymore. For the first time I could remember, I saw putting myself second as a good thing."

She had been holding her emotions in check up until now. But at this point they got the better of her and tears began to roll down her cheeks.

"Everything I went through with my parents cut me. And that cut was so deep, I thought nothing good could ever reach it. But when I fell in love with you, I felt it deeper than anything I had ever felt. That love was the first good thing to ever reach as deep as that pain. And it changed the way I saw everything. It brought me back to life. I didn't just fall in love with you. That love made me finally believe that something could be more powerful than pain. And in the middle of all this, it still is."

She released one hand and used it to wipe the tears from her eyes. I stood speechless for a moment. I had never heard her be so honest and vulnerable, and it made me love her even more.

"Wow," I chuckled. "I'm not really sure how to follow that."

She returned my laugh as she wiped another tear away.

"Ok. Here goes. I'm not as good with the words as you are, but I'll try."

I hesitated for a moment. What could I say that would measure up to the Shakespearean level monologue she had just delivered? Of course, there was nothing. All I could do is tell her how I felt.

"I love you, Charlie. You're strong. You're beautiful. You're like my roadmap, showing me which way is the right way. Life is hard, and I've never really been very good at figuring out what I want to be. But with you, life doesn't really seem so big and difficult. I see the way you look at me and I just don't understand it. In your face I see this admiration that looks like it's meant for a super hero. And I feel like I can never earn that look, but I want to, so bad. I can't really explain it, but I look at you and I…I see what I want to become."

I felt like I was rambling a little but she seemed to get the point. A smile reached across her face as the tears continued rolling down her cheeks.

I returned her smile as I finished, "There is no one that I would rather be with, here at the end of the world."

I leaned in and planted a kiss on her lips which caused her to giggle.

"Hey now," she said, "we haven't gotten to that part yet!"

"Oh, right," I remembered.

She started scanning the living room for something.

"What can we use as rings?" she asked.

Immediately I had an idea. I let go of her hands, held up a finger and retreated to the kitchen. I returned a few seconds later with a black permanent marker.

"You always said you wanted a tattoo wedding ring," I said as I removed the cap from the marker and took hold of her left hand.

I carefully drew the shape of a lotus blossom just above the base of her ring finger, and then two interwoven bands encircling the rest of her finger and connecting with the flower on either side.

"If I remember correctly, this is the design you had in mind."

"It's perfect!" she exclaimed as she examined it. "My turn."

She excitedly grabbed the marker and my left hand. She drew a similar, albeit better quality, design on my finger. Instead of two thinner interwoven bands, she drew a single thicker band, and instead of a lotus, she drew a rose. Before I could ask why she had made that choice, she looked up from her artwork and into my eyes.

"For Shayra," she whispered.

A lump formed in my throat at the words. My sister should have been here for this, but a tribute to her memory would have to be good enough.

"For Shayra," I repeated.

Charlie smiled and took another deep breath.

"Do you, Alexander Lee, take me, Charlotte Onasis, to be your wife?" she said ceremoniously.

"I do," I answered. "And do you, Charlotte Onasis, take me, Alexander Lee, to be your husband?"

"Heck yes!" she exclaimed. "Ok, now by the power vested in me by…also me, I guess, I pronounce us husband and wife. Now you can kiss me!"

She leapt at me so unexpectedly that I almost didn't catch her. Her arms wrapped around the back of my neck and her feet came entirely off the ground as she pulled me into a kiss. I returned her embrace and slowly lowered her back down to the floor. After a few moments she reluctantly pulled away.

"One more thing," she said with a twinkle in her eye.

"What?" I asked.

"We can't forget our first dance as a married couple!"

She reached for the remote that she had strategically placed within arms reach and pointed it towards the sound bar mounted below the TV. “Monsters” by Katie Sky started playing through the speakers.

“Our song,” I observed.

“What else?” she laughed.

I pulled her close as the memories flooded my mind. I picked up the remote, and with two button presses I set the song to repeat. I couldn’t bare the thought of our dance ending. Not yet. I wanted this moment to last as long as possible.

As we softly swayed back and forth in that living room in the middle of Oklahoma City, the concerns of the last few days faded away. There was no Lykos. There were no nano-organism. There was no clock reminding us how little time we had left. Instead, there was only us, lost in a perfect moment. Perhaps one of the last perfect moments that this version of the world would ever know.

32

Tuesday, April 27th, 2032

I stood in the kitchen of Charlie's Aunt and Uncle's house, sipping on the mornings second cup of coffee. I had gone through the first one in a matter of minutes and could tell quickly that it wasn't going to be enough. I spent most of the night restlessly tossing and turning, just like every night since my sister died. Every time I closed my eyes, I saw her lying in that hospital bed. The dream always ended the same way. Even now, as the sun crept up over the front of the house and the fog of sleep over my mind began to dissipate, I could still hear her voice in my head.

"What have you done?" she would say. *"You've killed them all!"*

And then it would all fall away and I would find myself staring at the ceiling or the wall, trying to slow my elevated breathing and heart rate.

Last night's sleeplessness was also owed to the many questions inherent to what we were trying to accomplish. And with every passing moment, those questions were multiplying. We had searched nearly half of the city's museums and felt no closer to finding the Lykos cloning facility. And beyond that, I couldn't even begin to imagine what I was supposed to do when we found it. I'm not a scientist, and I didn't really expect to find a copy of *Cloning for Dummies* lying around on a shelf. And how was I supposed to keep the clones from becoming infected? They couldn't survive without me, but if I was there when they were born they would be dead in forty-eight hours.

I lowered my head towards my coffee cup and took a deep breath.

Shayra would know the answer to every one of those questions. She always knew.

Thoughts about my sister never really changed. The fond remembrance followed closely by the sharp reality of her absence. It was, however, getting easier to shake off the bad thoughts. Even more so this morning.

Because this morning, even if just for a moment, everything was good.

Charlie had been awake before me. I'm not sure just how long she was up before I finally rolled out of the guest room bed, but it was at least long enough to start the generator, make coffee, and go for a swim. The sun hadn't finished rising and the temperature had not yet climbed above sixty-five degrees, and yet her form could clearly be seen through the sparkling water, moving swiftly from one side of the pool to the other.

My wife is quite the swimmer.

A smile crossed my face as I repeated the thought to myself.

My wife.

I watched out the window as she climbed up the steps to exit the pool. The new sunlight glistened off of the water droplets that trickled down from her hair to her shoulders. As she blotted her hair with the towel she had left on a nearby chair, I wondered if the bathing suit she was wearing had also belonged to her aunt, or if she had prepared to spend some time at a house with a pool. I decided the former was more likely since she hadn't been carrying around any luggage. However, with Charlie, you really never knew. Her behavior always seemed so chaotic, but after a while you would figure out that she had really been one step ahead of you the whole time. And by the time you had caught up, she was doing something else that wouldn't make sense until later. Eventually I just learned to go with it.

I realized when our eyes met through the kitchen window that I had been watching her quite intensely. Instinctively, I bounced my eyes away. When I looked back, she was laughing. I felt my face flush as I stepped through the dining room to meet her on the patio.

"You know, you're allowed to stare," she said flirtatiously as soon as I swung the back door open and stepped outside. "We're married now."

There was no suppressing a smile for either of us. We moved closer until we met near the edge of the pool. She leaned in and planted a kiss on my lips, giving no regard to the fact that she was saturating my freshly laundered clothes with the water from her bathing suit.

"Good morning," she said softly as she leaned back from the kiss, keeping her arms wrapped around my waist.

"Yes, it is," I replied, my grin growing even more.

Reluctantly we released our embrace so that she could finish drying off before entering the house.

"Why are you out here swimming when it's so cold?" I asked.

"Swimming in cold water is actually really good for you!" she shot back. "It boosts your immune system, helps with your circulation, plus it releases extra endorphins because it pushes you right to that pain threshold, you know? And so your body releases the endorphins to help you deal with the extra pain and—"

She stopped abruptly and I realized it was because of the inquisitive look on my face.

"What?" she said indignantly. "You think you're the only one who learned science stuff from Shayra?"

I shook my head and chuckled before turning back towards the house. "Yeah, that all sounds like something she would say. One time she spent about thirty minutes explaining to me why you're actually *not* more likely to survive a lightning strike if you're wearing rubber souled shoes after we watched *The Shawshank Redemption*."

"Really? Why?"

"I don't know, I guess that scene near the end where he's standing out in the rain—"

"No, dork, why are you not more likely to survive?"

"Oh. She said that rubber doesn't conduct electricity but only up to a certain point. The amount of rubber on shoes is only enough to protect you from like forty thousand volts. A lightning bolt is something like a billion."

"Wow. I'm really not sure what to do with that information."

"Me either. But I think maybe breakfast is the best course of action."

"Heck yes," she said with an enthusiastic nod before we turned to walk back towards the house, with her trailing a foot or two behind me.

"Oh," she added as we entered the kitchen, "she also explained to me why people put cucumber slices on their eyes during spa treatments and such. They have some kind of chemicals that help with…"

Her sentence trailed off just before a loud crash behind me caused me to spin around quickly. Charlie was on her knees on the kitchen floor and the knuckles on her right hand were white from gripping the edge of the counter. The coffee pot lay on its side next to her hand, coffee spilling across the counter and onto the floor.

"Are you ok?" I asked frantically as I reached to help her stand.

For a moment, she didn't seem to know what had happened any more than I did. She stared straight ahead and blinked furiously, as if she was trying to control the movement of the room.

"I uh…I don't know…" she managed as she slowly pushed herself back to standing. "I just lost my balance and when I tried to grab on to the counter, I hit the coffee pot. I don't know what happened. Just a bit of a dizzy spell, I guess."

Suddenly her gaze locked onto mine and I could tell from the mixture of panic and sadness in her eyes that we had just had the same realization. We both knew exactly what had happened, but neither of us would dare say it out loud.

"I'm going to go get dressed," she said abruptly. "We can eat breakfast in the car."

Without another word from either of us, she turned and walked briskly towards the bedroom. The reality that I had been suppressing for the last ten hours was back at the forefront of my mind.

We were running out of time.

33

The Oklahoma Black Museum and the Oklahoma Sports Hall of Fame were both less than a mile from the house where we were staying and so we decided to start there. It was a long shot that the cloning facility would be located in either, but we had to be thorough. By 10:00 a.m. we had searched both, as well as Harn Homestead, the southern most museum in the area, and had looped back north to the Oklahoma History Center. The History Center was probably the largest facility we would have to search. It was eighteen acres of exhibits, collection, event facilities, and a research center.

Charlie and I got a little excited when we saw that last one on the map just outside the gift shop, but it turned out to be merely a collection of historical databases and indexes rather than any kind of scientific facility. Searching the history center ate up the rest of the morning and by noon we had decided to return to the house for lunch before continuing on to the four remaining locations to the north-east.

We sat in the living room of Charlie's Aunt's and Uncle's house, each of us slouched into our respective seats. Two half eaten plates of sautéed sausage and potatoes sat on the coffee table between us. I was finding it difficult to not let the discouragement about our lack of progress effect my countenance. I was staring at the leftover food on my plate and unsuccessfully trying to suppress a frown.

Charlie, however, had managed to channel her disappointment into determination. She had pushed her food to the other side of the table and perched herself on the edge of the couch, with the remaining brochures we had collected from the art museum spread across the space her plate had previously occupied. She was leaning forward with her elbows resting on her knees rubbing her temples, as if to massage her thoughts into place.

"So what exactly did Patrick say?" she asked.

I sat up just enough to not seem disinterested in the conversation. "I told him that Shayra didn't give me the location of the cloning facility in her letter. He said that wasn't a surprise because most people didn't even know about the project much less where it was located. And then he started thinking out loud and said 'I wonder if that's what they set up in that old museum.'"

Her head shot up. "*Old* museum?"

"Yeah, I'm pretty sure that's what he said."

"He had to mean one that wasn't in operation anymore."

I sat up further in my seat. I hadn't even made that connection until that moment.

"So it can't be any of these," she said, motioning towards the brochures on the table. "We're looking for a building that *used* to be a museum."

I sank back into my seat at this new revelation.

"Any building in this town could have been a museum at some point!" I groaned.

"Yeah," she started rubbing her temples again, "but this would have to be one that closed recently. With what you've told me, Lykos wouldn't have wanted to waste a bunch of money fixing up an old, decrepit building. And they would probably want somewhere that already had some facilities they could make use of for the sake of saving money on—"

Without warning she jumped to her feet.

"Alex!" she said, her eyes wide with excitement. "The Science Museum."

"The Science Museum was one of my favorite places when I was a kid," Charlie explained as we walked to our respective sides of the Range Rover. "I used to go there all the time when I was younger. But then they closed it down right before I moved to Fort Worth."

"So that would have been about three or four years ago?" I asked.

"Yeah, something like that. It was right around the time AllianceHealth bought that nursing home right down the street from the museum. I was there almost every day for a couple of months helping re-train the other nurse's assistants. One day, I drove by and the parking lot of the museum was just empty. Come to think of it, I don't even remember seeing a for-sale sign."

"Lykos must have snatched it up before anybody else had a chance. Or worse, they bought it first and then shut it down."

"That has to be the place," she concluded excitedly. "It totally makes sense."

I buckled my seatbelt and pressed the start button, causing the engine to roar to life.

"Still," I added with a sarcastic smile, "it's kind of a shame that we won't get to see the pigeon museum."

I shifted into drive and pulled out of the circle drive on to Willard.

"Turn right up here at 50th," she instructed.

"How far is it?"

"Just a mile or two." She leaned her head against the window so she could see the darkening clouds gathering overhead. "And good thing too. Looks like the weather is about to get nasty."

"Yeah, and we're incredibly low on—"

Before I could finish, the Range Rover's engine began to sputter. Charlie and I exchanged a panicked look just before the vehicle shuddered and every light on the dashboard lit up. We rolled to a stop just before reaching the intersection.

"Was there a gas can at the house?" Charlie asked without skipping a beat.

"No good," I shook my head. "There was one, but I emptied it into the generator last night."

I scanned the driveways of the houses around us for any easily accessible vehicles that may have at least a partially full tank of gas, but I saw none.

"Should we check one of these houses, see if any of them has a car in the garage?" I suggested.

She also briefly scanned the street before shaking her head. "Why don't we just walk. It's not too far."

"Uh, yeah, ok," I said, looking once again at the bulging clouds above us. "I guess we're walking."

I climbed out of the vehicle and jogged to the back end to retrieve the shotgun I had stowed there, and then over to her side to open the door.

"What a gentleman," she teased as she slid out of the seat.

I took a few steps towards the intersection, but quickly noticed that Charlie wasn't beside me. I turned to see her standing by the front of the Range Rover with her left hand resting on the hood, seemingly to maintain her balance. She had her head down and eyes closed.

"Are you ok?" I already knew the answer.

She raised her head and forced her eyes open.

"Yep, I'm good," she stated confidently.

Although it seemed that she said it more to convince herself than me. I offered my hand for support and she reluctantly accepted. She was not really one to ask for help so I knew I would have to take the initiative. As we walked arm in arm passed the stop sign at Willard and 50th, I felt the first raindrop hit my head.

34

We made it about half way to the Oklahoma Science Museum before the rainfall became too heavy and we were forced to take shelter under the covered porch of a small church just off of the main road. We sat on the concrete stoop with our backs up against the double glass doors. There were six feet of concrete between us and the water pouring off the edges of the overhang on each side. The downpour was so thick, we could barely make out the shape of the house on the opposite side of the street from us.

"I've always loved the rain," Charlie mused as we watched it fall. "There's just something cathartic about it, you know?"

"Yeah," I muttered, "unless you are trying to walk somewhere."

"We'll get there soon enough. For now, I just want to enjoy this."

It suddenly occurred to me that this would probably be the last rainstorm she would ever see. I had become so focused on the destination that I had forgotten that every passing moment was one of our last moments together. I decided to make better use of this unexpected pause in our journey.

"So," I started as lightheartedly as I could manage, "what's one of your favorite memories of us?"

"Besides our wedding?" she answered sarcastically.

"Yeah, that would be too easy."

"Let's see," she said thoughtfully. "I would have to say the day we met. At Craftwork."

"That is a good one. I can't believe that was your first time there. Must have been fate or something that I stopped and talked to you."

A knowing smile crept across her lips.

"Um, yeah," she said hesitantly. "Now that you mention it, there is a part of that story that you don't know."

I leaned away from the glass and turned to look her in the eyes.

"That wasn't my first time there," she confessed. "I had actually been there a couple dozen times."

"What? You told me that was your first time!"

"Well, actually, no I didn't. You said 'This must be your first time in here because I'm in here all the time and I'm sure I would've noticed you.' I just didn't correct you."

"Wow. Ok. I think that still counts as a lie but I guess I'll let it slide. Why wouldn't you just say you had been there before?"

"Well, to be honest I was afraid that would lead to a longer discussion and I would end up having to tell you the truth."

"Which is?"

"I did see you there the first time I came in, but you didn't see me. So I kept coming back, hoping I would see you again."

"Seriously? You came back looking for me? Why?"

She chuckled softly as she watched the rain fall, "I guess there was just something about you. Something I couldn't really make myself forget."

"Huh. So I guess you did eventually see me again?"

"Yep. I came and got coffee every day for almost a week before I saw you again."

"And that was the day we met?"

"Well, no, not exactly. I spent the whole time waiting to see if you would notice me, but instead you left without saying a word. So every time after that, I sat at the table in the front corner by the door."

"And that's when I finally noticed you?"

She laughed. "No, after a while I decided that if I was going to be spending that much time sitting around a coffee shop I should at least bring something to read. The first day I sat down with that book in my hands was the day you finally came over and talked to me."

I shook my head in unbelief and leaned back against the glass door. "Wow. I guess I'm lucky that you're persistent once you decide you want something. Otherwise, we probably never would have met."

She leaned her head over and rested it on my shoulder.

"I'm the lucky one," she said softly.

Her head rested at the perfect level for the smell of her hair to waft up towards my nose. Somehow, even after several days and multiple showers, the distinct smell of dragon fruit was still unmistakable.

The moment flooded me with a bittersweetness like I had never experienced. The rain carried with it a freshness, reminding me of our new start. I found myself lost in the soft rhythm of her breathing. All I wanted to do was to dream about our future together. To imagine the days when all our years were spent building a life. When we had given our best, and even our worst days to each other, only to find that even better days lay ahead. But those days, those years, and that life could never be.

"I don't understand you two," I said after a moment.

"Who?" she said, lifting her head off of my shoulder.

"You and Shayra. It seems like all I've done my whole life is screw up and yet the two of you still believe in me somehow."

"Of course we believe in you. Alex, you are capable of far more than the tiny bit of credit you give yourself."

"But what if I'm not?"

"What do you mean?"

"Shayra trusted me with this huge thing. What if she got the wrong guy? What if…what if I can't do it? What if all this has been for nothing and this really is the end of everything?"

She paused for a long moment. I could tell she was looking for the right words.

"Alex, six months ago I had to walk away from our relationship. That was the right thing for me to do and I stand by that decision. But look at us now. Look at you and everything you've overcome to be here right now. When I left, I never believed it was the end for us. Because even through all your mistakes, there is one thing about you that never fails. No matter how long it takes, or how many lessons you have to learn along the way, in the end you always come through for the people you care about. That's what we see in you. And that's why I know you can do this."

There was no lie in Charlie's eyes. She believed every word of what she just said. I reached up to discretely wipe the moisture from my eyes, but there was no hiding it. Without another word she gently turned my face towards hers and pulled me in for a kiss.

"So let's go do it," she said intently after she pulled away.

She stood to her feet and vigorously brushed off the back of her jeans.

"Shall we?" she offered, motioning towards the rain that was now barely a sprinkle.

As I stood to join her, a distant sound arrested our attention. I picked out the sound of at least two beasts, most likely dogs of some kind, snarling and whimpering in what sounded like a fight to the death.

"Yeah," I said as I reached for Charlie's hand, "I think it's best that we do."

35

About twenty minutes later, we were in the parking lot of the convenience store at the corner of 50th and MLK Ave, looking towards the rear side of the Oklahoma Science Museum. It was an L shaped building with a large parking lot for patrons on the north side, just across from the main entrance. Even though the museum hadn't been in operation for years, the main entrance was still securely locked. However, the butt end of my shotgun proved to be an effective way to bypass the glass doors. Once inside, I noticed a manual gate that could be pulled down from the ceiling for an extra layer of protection.

Recalling the noises we had heard a few minutes before, I decided pulling the gate down was the best course of action. As it clattered into place, Charlie gave me a nod to indicate she understood my reasoning. We walked past the reception desk and the theatre box office towards the main exhibit floor which, thanks to Lykos, was now completely empty.

"I can't imagine a top secret facility being in any of these big open spaces like this," I said just above a whisper. "We're probably looking for some sort of employee area."

"Or maybe a basement," Charlie said at full volume as she pointed to a white metal door about twenty feet away.

An illustration of a man walking down stairs adorned the plastic sign next to it. At the bottom of the staircase, we found another nondescript white door, this time with no handle. A small grey rectangle panel next to the door, like the one at Western Place, indicated the only method of entry was some sort of badge or key fob. A small red light below the RF panel indicated the facility was still running on some kind of backup power, just like the security system at The Museum of Art.

My heart leapt when I noticed the insignia above the panel. It was less than an inch in diameter and the name had been omitted, but the logo was unmistakable.

"Lykos," I whispered. "This is it. It has to be."

I turned to Charlie for agreement, but what I saw in her eyes was immeasurable pride. She was practically beaming.

"It has to be," she repeated with a catch in her voice.

I pulled Shayra's teardrop shaped key fob from my pocket and pressed it against the panel. It let out a beep just like the one at the lab, but instead of turning green, the red light below it gave three quick orange flashes and then returned to red.

My smile disappeared. I flashed Charlie a quick glance and saw that hers had as well. I pressed on the door with my palm, but it didn't budge.

"I don't understand," I said as I pressed the key fob against the panel again, with the same results.

"I guess she didn't have clearance for this place," Charlie said casually.

I shook my head. "That can't be right. She had full clearance. At least that's what they told her. Why would they want to keep her out of here?"

"Who knows? These people are crazy."

"So? What do we do?"

Charlie rolled her eyes at me. As usual, she already had a plan and it involved absolutely no forethought. She pulled the shotgun off of my shoulder and over my head, the strap scraping my nose as it passed by. Before I could react she had already chambered a round.

"Charlie! Don't—" I yelled.

But it was too late. The powerful resonance of the shotgun blast in the tiny stairwell left my ears ringing and my head throbbing. She shoved the weapon back in my direction, smoke still fuming from the barrel.

"There we go," I knew she said, not because I could hear it over the ringing in my ears, but only because I read her lips.

With the impact of the blast, the door had given way and now stood open, revealing nothing more than darkness.

"We need to find a light switch," I yelled as I slung the shotgun back over my shoulder.

"What?" she yelled back.

I pantomimed the action of flipping on a light switch. She nodded and then gave me a quick thumbs up. I was expecting some sort of huge master switch like in the movies to crank everything up, but what I found was a simple household light switch.

The fluorescent lights flickered to life, slowly illuminating the room one section at a time. I estimated the main lab area to be about six hundred square feet, and a quick scan told me it was only one of at least four areas in the facility. A door on the wall far to the left was labeled "*Incubation,*" on the wall opposite the entrance was a door that read "*Storage,*" and lastly, on a door on the right wall was a plastic sign that read "*Quarantine.*"

The lab area was bordered by cabinets and counters that were all immaculately kept, much like Shayra's lab at Western Place. Except unlike hers, these were stainless steel. It gave this lab a cold and clinical feel and made the various machines and equipment placed around the room seem much more menacing.

In the center of the room was the most interesting piece of equipment. A circular, metal sort of bowl, almost the size and shape of a bird bath, stood with room all around it for someone to stand, with freestanding cabinets a distance away on each side. Above it was a metal arm with multiple joints so that it could be pulled down towards the bowl or pushed up out of the way. At the end of the arm was a metal needle. Not the kind used for injections, but more akin to a giant record player.

While considering its use, a computer monitor mounted to the back wall caught my attention.

"That looks like a good place to start," I said, pointing to the screen.

We made our way over to the console, and with a tap on the screen, the words "*Authorization Required*" appeared in white on the otherwise vacant darkness of the screen. If Shayra was correct, the password that would grant us entry was my name. I looked around for a keyboard or some other way to input the password, but found none.

"How am I supposed to put in the password?" I thought out loud. "There's no keyboard."

Charlie studied the screen for a moment.

"It's probably voice activated," she said. "You said the password to the whole system is your name, right?"

"That's what Shayra's letter said."

She leaned in slightly towards the screen.

"Alexander," she tried.

Suddenly the screen went blank.

"Authorization accepted," a computerized female voice announced through the speakers in the ceiling.

With that, the entire lab came to life. A complicated looking user interface appeared on the computer monitor in front of us and the machines around the room began to light up and make various beeping and whirring noises.

Charlie shot a cheesy grin my way. I shook my head in near disbelief.

"She did it," I said with a chuckle. "I can't believe she really did it. She gave us a backdoor into the entire system."

"I can't believe she had that kind of access," Charlie mused while we watched the room powering up.

"I guess she was more important to Lykos than she let on," I responded.

"I guess so. I bet that's why they had somebody watching her room at the hospital."

"Probably. They wouldn't have wanted—" I stopped mid-sentence as a realization hit me.

"I never told you that," I said slowly as I turned to face her. "How did you know about that?"

Her eyes grew wide for a fraction of a second before she returned to a forced casual expression. "Of course you did. I'm sure you just don't remember."

"No, I didn't. How did you know that?"

I took a step towards her and she recoiled slightly.

"Alex, come on, is it really that big of a deal? Does it matter—"

"Charlie," I said sharply, "tell me."

Her eyes darted across my face, down to my feet, and back to my face again. She was desperately looking for a way out of the conversation, but there was nowhere else for her to go. She took a deep breath and let out a heavy sigh before she finally conceded.

"Shayra called me," she admitted.

36

"She what?" I said as my countenance softened.

That was not the answer I was expecting. I had almost began to think Charlie was somehow working for Lykos. But this felt worse.

My anger melted quickly into hurt. "Why would you keep that from me?"

She didn't answer but rather looked at me with a unique mixture of compassion and guilt.

"Is this why you went into that quarantine room?" I pressed.

"Alex, I'm sorry," was all she could manage. "She said it would be best if we didn't tell you."

"What? What could you possibly have had to talk about that I couldn't know?"

"No, it wasn't like that! She told me about the nano-organisms and how it was the end of the world. She told me about her plan and said…"

"What? What did she say?"

She hesitated once more before letting out another deep sigh. "She said that you couldn't do it without my help."

My heart sank. All this time, it was my sister's belief in me that kept me going. It was what drove me on and made me feel like maybe I could do something like this. But in the end it was all a lie. My sister didn't believe in me. She believed in Charlie.

"I see," I said softly as I looked towards the ground, partly to hide the tears forming in my eyes, but also because I couldn't look at Charlie without the searing pain in my gut growing more intense. "Yes, that makes sense. Anything else I should know?"

"Alex—"

"Did she say anything else?" I repeated forcefully.

"No. You know how she is in situations like that. She was all business. Said she had a lot of planning to do so we just said our goodbyes and hung up."

I simply nodded.

"Look," I choked out, "I know we have a lot of work to do, but I just need a little air so I'm going to step outside for a second and then you can, uh, you can *help* me with all of this."

"Alex, that's not what she meant. Alex, wait!" she called after me.

But I didn't. I couldn't. I had to get away from her. Right now she only served as a reminder that every encouraging word my sister ever told me was a lie. Everything inside of me was crumbling. Everything I had believed about this plan and about myself was unraveling.

I roughly lifted the gate that blocked the front entrance of the Science Museum and stepped through the doorway, unsure of what to do or where to go. Even the filtered sunlight breaking through the dissipating rain clouds made my eyes burn as they struggled to adapt to the quick transition from the dim light of the lab.

I needed something. A distraction. Something to drink, maybe. The convenience store across the street caught my eye. That would do the trick. As I reached the street, I heard Charlie's voice calling out behind me.

"Alex!" she shouted.

I didn't have anything to say to her right now. At least, nothing that I wouldn't regret later. Nonetheless she persisted, following me across the street and into the convenience store parking lot. I was passing in front of the large glass windows that stretched the length of the storefront when she finally caught up to me.

"Alex, stop!" she said as she grabbed my shoulder and spun me to face her. "You don't understand."

"I think I understand just fine," I answered sarcastically. "My sister knew I couldn't pull this off so she planted you here to keep an eye on me so I wouldn't screw this up like I do everything else. Like I did when I started this whole thing. Did I miss anything?"

"Yes, you did."

"Oh yeah, you're right." I paused for a second to collect my emotions that, at that moment, were on the verge of a full break. "I didn't even get to tell my sister goodbye. But you did."

I didn't wait for a response, but instead turned to walk away. I only made it three or four steps before her words made me stop.

"Shayra knew you better than anybody," she explained. "And I promise you that she believed in you more than you'll ever know. It was you who didn't."

I turned slowly to face her, still trying to keep the tears forming in my eyes from falling.

"Don't you get it?" she continued. "She knew the only reason you ever thought you could accomplish anything was because she was there to encourage you and push you forward. She told me there was nothing she wanted more desperately than to be able to do that for you. But she couldn't. And so she called me. Not because she didn't believe you could do this, but because she knew that *you* would never believe you could."

A single tear broke free and rolled down my cheek. It was always my sister's encouragement that kept me going. Even through so much of this ordeal, it was the only thing I had to hold on to.

"You never needed anybody to help you do this," she added softly. "You just needed somebody to help you believe you could. And that was a task that I was happy to accept."

We stood in silence for a long while. Sufficient words failed me. I didn't want to believe her. Everything in my head wanted to hang on to the hurt, but I couldn't. I knew she was right. I knew Shayra was right. I needed Charlie for this, even if it was just to have someone who believed in me. I should've known my sister knew what she was doing.

My self reflection was short lived, as a guttural sound nearby shattered it. In the heat of our fight, a beast of some kind had managed to approach undetected. I turned as quickly as I dared, resisting the urge to make any kind of swift movement. A battle-wounded Rottweiler stood less than ten feet away, snarling through blood stained fangs. His muscular body was already poised in an attack position, ready to sprint without warning at his prey.

And his eyes were fixed on me.

37

The impact came unexpectedly, not from the front, but from the side. Just before the animal launched itself in my direction, I reached for the shotgun strapped to my back. I knew I didn't have time to chamber a round, much less get it in firing position before the attack came, but it was the only thing I could think to do in the moment. I heard Charlie scream my name just before my hand clutched the handle of the weapon that hung behind my back. Before I could move it into position, I felt her hands push me and I began to fall.

Then, as I fell, it felt as if time slowed. I turned my head just in time to see the Rottweiler's front paws catch Charlie just below the neck. My hands frantically reached through the ever increasing space between us, trying to get to her. But I was completely helpless as I watched her and the beast crash through the thick glass window on the front of the convenience store.

My shoulders impacted hard on the concrete. That sudden jolt was enough to bring time back into proportion. I struggled to get to my feet, at the same time trying to process what had just happened.

"Charlie," I muttered out loud.

I turned towards the sound of the snarling dog and the sound of her screams. The Rottweiler had a hold of her by the ankle and was dragging her back and forth across the shards of glass and the dingy tile floor of the convenience store. I quickly searched the area for the shotgun which, by this time, lay several feet away. I picked it up and chambered a round while aiming it towards the animal's head.

It was no use. There was no shot I could take without hitting Charlie. I had to think of something else before it was too late, even as the thought that it may already be too late fought for control of my mind.

I searched for something, anything that could be used as a weapon. As I did, I refused to let it register on my mind that among the snarling and growling I could no longer hear Charlie screaming.

She reached up with her free hand and aggressively gripped my sleeve.

"No, Alex," she said, an ever growing panic in her now glistening eyes. "I can't move my legs."

"You can't—" My voice caught as a lump rose up in my throat.

I looked up and down her body. It didn't take long to figure out that one of the shards of glass had probably damaged her spinal cord as the Rottweiler dragged her across the floor.

I opened my mouth to speak, but couldn't produce any sounds. There were no words for this moment. Nothing could fix it. Nothing could undo it.

"Alex," she said between shallow breaths, "remember what we talked about. Don't be sad."

My face contorted with emotion as I shook my head, "Charlie, no. This can't happen. We have more time. We have to. We haven't even—we—"

She looked directly into my eyes as a single tear rolled down her cheek. I leaned in closer to her face.

"We were supposed to have more time," I said softly as tears began to roll down my cheeks as well.

"I love you, Alex," she whispered.

"I love you too," I said through tears.

I leaned in and gave her a kiss, knowing full well that it would be our last. As I pulled away, I noticed a pool of purple-tinted blood already forming underneath where she lay.

I searched frantically in my mind for something I could say. Something I could do.

Charlie worked in the medical field. Maybe she could talk me through some kind of procedure or fix. Maybe I could still save her.

"What do I do?" I asked, my voice thick with emotion.

Her breathing was becoming more labored and her grip on my sleeve began to relax. She gave her head a gentle shake.

"Charlie, what do I do?" I repeated, shouting through sobs.

"Oh, Alex…" she said, clearly struggling to manage a weak smile.

With the last of her strength, she reached up and ran her fingers across my cheek.

"Go and save the world," she whispered fiercely.

With that, I felt her muscles relax and her body fall limp in my arms. I pulled her close in a desperate embrace and collapsed into her chest.

38

I spent the rest of the afternoon digging a shallow grave in the grassy area behind the small church two lots down from the convenience store on MLK Avenue. I had lost too many people without being able to say a proper goodbye and I refused to let Charlie be just one more. She had saved my life by giving hers. I would give her the send off that she deserved.

A newly built organic produce store occupied the lot between the convenience store and the church. Inside, where I hoped to find some kind of flowers, I found instead a display of fresh dragon fruit. I placed several of them next to her in the hole I had dug. I ran my fingers through her silver blue hair one more time after I placed the last one.

By the time I had finished, the sun was just beginning to set. I rested in the grass next to the pile of dirt that now covered my wife, absentmindedly picking pieces of grass and then releasing them for the wind to carry away. The rain clouds had mostly passed, but still the world felt dark and overcast. A world without Charlie was something I would never have hoped to see.

"You saved my life, you know," I said out loud as if she could hear me. "I didn't really get to say thank you for that. Just like I never got to say goodbye to Shayra. Or my parents, or Patrick, or even Shelly."

I released another pinch of grass into the wind.

"Maybe that's just how life is, you know? Maybe you never really get to say everything you need to say. Maybe you just have to live it the best you can and then say the rest at the funeral."

I turned and looked at the mound of dirt next to me, "Ok. I'll do the best I can."

I cleared my throat and straightened my back.

"Charlie," I started, "you were the most amazing human being I ever met. You never waited to act long enough that fear had a chance to catch up to you. You lived your life and didn't ask for anybody's permission to do so. Your hair was always colorful."

I shook my head and looked back at the grass in front of me. Every word I said felt so flat and insignificant. I took a deep breath and decided to stop trying to be poetic.

"The truth is that everything about you was amazing. But what made you really amazing was what I became when I was with you. When you left, I lost that. I lost the best part of me and I felt like such a failure. But then I saw you standing there through the door of that quarantine room. And when I saw you, I forgot what it felt like to be a failure. And then when I touched you, I forgot what it felt like to be afraid. And when I kissed you I forgot…I forgot everything. Everything except you."

I closed my eyes as a gust of wind blew against my face. The lingering petrichor prevailed itself on my senses as I allowed the tears to roll down my cheeks once more.

"And I won't forget you. I can't. Because every time I'm brave and every time I keep going, I'll think of you."

I looked up towards the sky and attempted to blink back the tears. When that was unsuccessful, I used my shirt to blot the moisture from my eyes. The wind began to pick up as another round of storm clouds was forming to the west. By now the sun had nearly finished setting and without power to the street lights I could barely see the grass by my feet swaying in the wind.

I wished I had it in me to deliver a heartfelt and meaningful eulogy to everyone I had ever known, but I was utterly and completely spent. I knew I needed to go, but I couldn't bring myself to leave just yet. Instead I laid back in the grass and watched as the evening's first stars began to appear.

Don't fall asleep.

When we were kids, Shayra and I used to lie out on the trampoline in our backyard while she told me the names of the stars and constellations. With the buildings and street lights gone, more stars were visible than I had ever seen before.

"You should be here to see these stars, Shay," I mused out loud. "I bet you would know the name of every single one of them."

A cool breeze swept across my face as my eyelids began to feel heavy.

Don't fall asleep, Alex.

The world around me grew darker as I breathed in the scent of the approaching rain.

"You should be here," I whispered again as consciousness finally slipped away.

I awoke to a raindrop on my face. Then another. And another. I used my arms to push myself up to a sitting position, shaking off the feelings inherent to a bad dream.

You fell asleep.

I scanned the area to try and get my bearings. Everything was dark. Had I actually had a bad dream? How long had I slept? Any light that had been emanating from the moon or stars was now blocked by cloud cover. I groped in the dark until my hand landed on the fresh pile of dirt. My breath caught as the familiar sting of loss permeated my entire being. It hadn't been a bad dream at all. It was all painfully real.

The moonlight broke through the clouds just enough to make out the shape of the Science Museum building across the street.

You have a job to do. Charlie would want you to keep moving.

My muscles protested sharply as I stood to my feet and brushed the dirt from my pant legs. Even as I did so, the blood stains remained as a potent reminder of what I had lost. I was now truly alone.

Don't be sad.

With shards of glass still embedded in my hand and Charlie's blood still staining my jeans, I turned my eyes to The Science Museum.

39

I pulled the gate that covered the front door of the museum down securely into position. With the glass on the front door broken and the door to the cloning area half destroyed by a shotgun blast, the last thing I needed was some creature wondering into the lab when I wasn't looking. Especially since the Oklahoma City Zoo was only a matter of feet outside the museum door.

Once back inside the lab, I couldn't even wrap my head around the task ahead of me. My thoughts kept returning to Charlie. Most of my energy was going to keeping those thoughts from causing a breakdown, while allowing them just enough to keep me motivated.

I decided that the best place to start was just to familiarize myself with the facility. I started with the storage area located at the back of the main lab. It was a decent sized area, I guessed about two hundred square feet, lined with shelves containing various supplies. On the top shelf, just inside the door to the right were about three dozen composition notebooks, like the ones from Shayra's lab, and five two inch thick binders. I had a feeling I would be spending a significant amount of time with both sets of documentation.

At the back of the storage room was a stainless steel door that closely resembled the door to a walk-in freezer at a restaurant. It was roughly four feet wide and eight feet high, with a handle on the right side secured with a cotter pin style lock. The plastic sign to the left of the door read "*Embryonic Storage.*"

"There's even a cryogenic storage unit onsite where they have already gathered the samples," I remembered the words from Shayra's letter.

That had to be it. Everything was exactly as she had said it would be. For the first time since I undertook this task, I felt like it might actually work.

Next, I made my way to the room labeled "*Incubation.*" I guessed I would be spending a good amount of time in here as well. The room seemed to go on forever, stretching beyond my sight into the dark. I ran my hand blindly across the wall until I found the light switch.

The moment the lights came on, a sense of uneasiness overcame me. Something wasn't right. The cloning pods were neatly arranged in ten rows of ten, for a total of a hundred pods. However, most of them appeared incomplete. Several had wires hanging out of panels on the side, several sat with the lids detached laying on the ground, and at least one that I could see had the entire outer shell lying in pieces nearby. From where I stood, I could only see one pod that appeared complete and ready. But that wasn't all that had unnerved me.

My mind moved on quickly to the size of the pods. Each one measured roughly ten feet in length, far too large for an infant. Maybe the tech inside took up most of that space? Maybe each pod could incubate more than one embryo?

I sprinted back to the storage area and started riffling through the composition notebooks. The sloppy handwriting on the cover of each book read "*Project Legion*" followed by numbers ranging from one through thirty-three. I flipped open book number one, hoping to find a summary of the project somewhere in the early pages. I found it on page three and began scanning until I located the data I needed.

And then, as I read the specs, I almost wished I hadn't:

Pod capacity: 1

Estimated incubation time: 7,300 days

40

Wednesday, May 5th, 2032

I spent the next eight days reading through every notebook on the shelf in the storage area and searching the internet for everything I could get ahold of on the subject of cloning. With power grids going out all over the world, I was finding fewer and fewer websites that were still reachable. I guessed those I could still access were the ones whose servers were located in areas that still had power or had some sort of backup power keeping them running, much like this facility. Between the thorough notes contained in the thirty-three composition notebooks and my online research, I came to see that the concept of cloning was not as mysterious and complicated as I had first imagined. The nucleus of a donor cell is transplanted into a host egg cell from which the original nucleus has been removed. It's transferred from there to a surrogate or, in this case a pod, for incubation.

Unfortunately, I didn't have even the beginnings of the knowledge needed to complete such a process. However, after reading the notebooks, I moved on to the binders and discovered that the various pieces of equipment I had seen around the lab had been designed to mostly automate said process.

A machine that resembled an espresso maker would artificially manufacture an already enucleated egg cell and deposit it in a small metal tube. Then another machine would take the DNA sample from the cryogenic storage and separate the nucleus from the donor cell, depositing it into another metal tube, identical to the first except with a different color coded label. To keep the embryos pure, each tube could be used only once before being discarded.

A third machine, akin in appearance to a childhood rock polisher, would combine the separated nucleus with the enucleated egg and deposit the embryo into a third metal tube. This tube would be inserted into a slot in the center of the final machine in the lab, the one that looked to me like a metal bird bath, where the articulating arm with the needle on the end would fuse the nucleus and the egg together using an electric shock, leaving it finally ready for incubation.

The process to prepare each embryo took around fourteen hours and, according to the copious amount of notes, they had completed it several times successfully, stopping just short of incubation. It seemed that the project was near completion and they were preparing for the time when the pods were up and running.

Among the one hundred cloning pods in the facility, I managed to locate one that was ready and operational, and one more that was near completion. The second pod had only a few final connections that needed to be soldered together before it was ready, so I decided to wait and initialize both at the same time.

Fortunately, one of the binders contained full instruction and schematics for the pods. Schematics that, thanks to my time at Lockheed Martin, I was able to read with minimal difficulty. Or I was at least able to tell what connections went where. As far as how everything actually worked, it was technology like I had never seen.

These pods were capable of so much more than just simple cloning. Before beginning the incubation process, you could select gender, hair color, or even height and the pod would make the necessary genome adjustments. Or you could allow it to randomize some or all characteristics, even within certain designated parameters.

Beyond that, if I was understanding the notes correctly, the pod could even implant information into the brain of the developing clone during incubation. According to the research in the notes, all knowledge and memory is basically created through synapsis firing in the brain. Using electric impulses and what they referred to as synapse control, the pods could basically "pre-load" clones with an education.

The more I learned about Project Legion, the less "clone" seemed like the appropriate term. This facility was not built simply to take a human DNA sample and recreate it. It was more like a farm for growing brand new, unique humans. It was man playing God.

The ethical implications were heavy, and if I had the time or option to consider them, I would have. Unfortunately the only two options that the world had left were these artificially created humans, or no humans at all. I convinced myself that it was no different than artificial insemination and left it at that.

I found a .38 caliber handgun in one of the drawers in the storage area, which afforded me the courage to venture outside the facility for food, now that all my shotgun rounds had been expended.

At first I would go across the street to the convenience store, but it didn't take long before the sight of the broken glass and dried blood on the floor became too much to handle. I found another small discount market down the street in a strip mall that was still close enough to walk. Each time I passed the church where Charlie was buried, memories would wash over me. Some days those memories would put a smile on my face, but most days it was just too fresh not to hurt.

I knew at some point, I would need to locate a vehicle and make a run to an actual grocery store, but for now, breakfast snack cakes and canned ravioli would have to suffice.

All the tools and parts I needed to complete the other ninety-nine pods were already here in the facility in an additional storage area off of the incubation room. Once I had thoroughly studied the schematic for the pod, it took me less than an hour to solder the remaining connections on the almost completed pod.

Two weeks to the day after my sister died, I stood ready to put her plan into action. I had read every book in the facility as well as every article online that I could access. If I would ever be ready to take on this task, it was now.

I had already prepared one embryo and had just finished administering the electric shock to fuse the nucleus and the egg of the second one. I felt my heartbeat beginning to accelerate as I carried both to the incubation room and inserted them into the appropriate slot in their respective pods.

On the first pod I selected male for the gender, and on the second I selected female. I loaded the former with a biochemistry education module, and the latter with botany. I decided those would be the most useful for the challenges they would face when they awoke. I left all other characteristics set to "random". They were one row and three pods apart so I was able to initiate the process on both within a few seconds of each other. A ten minute countdown appeared on the control panel screen of both pods along with a message.

Implanting embryo. Please stand by.

The Rose Contingency was officially under way. I didn't have much time to enjoy my victory. Before even a minute had elapsed on the countdown, a loud crash arrested my attention. I turned quickly towards the door and reached for the pistol I had tucked down the back of my jeans. After allowing my mind a moment to process, I determined that the crash was far too distant and muffled to have come from the lab area. Maybe something had fallen in the storage room?

I quickly made my way there, but on arrival found nothing out of place. There was only one option that remained. I had been here for over a week but hadn't yet bothered to check the quarantine room. But it was now inescapably clear that someone, or something, had been living in there since before I arrived.

41

It had been at least six months since the last time I had seen Dr. Gainsborough. Our past interactions in the Lykos halls had been so brief and inconsequential, I almost wasn't sure if he would even know who I was. He was kneeling down on the other side of a door composed of glass panels separated by white plastic crossbars, almost identical to the one I had found Charlie behind a few days before. In fact, I wondered if perhaps the parts had been acquired from that very same facility.

He was just finishing soaking up a coffee spill with a wad of paper towels when my movement seemed to register in the corner of his eye. He turned his head towards me, an expression of calm on his face. He seemed nearly unfazed by my presence. In fact, it almost seemed as if he had been expecting me.

"Mr. Lee," he said, maintaining the level of verbal decorum I had come to expect from him. "I was beginning to wonder if you would make it over to this part of the facility."

He stood and tossed the coffee soaked paper towels in a nearby trash can, before turning back towards me and adjusting his glasses.

He was dressed more casual than I had ever seen him and yet he still looked like he could be ready for some kind of board meeting at a moment's notice. He wore a medium gray dress shirt tucked into black dress slacks. Every part of his outfit, from his white hair to his leather soled dress shoes, was immaculately clean and well kept. It was also all clearly expensive. It was the kind of look that Mr. Kingston at Masterson P&P had always tried to pull off, but never really could.

He had already spotted the pistol in my right hand, but it seemed he found it more amusing than threatening.

"I heard you blast your way in to the lab eight days ago," he continued. "But there were two voices then. Where is the young lady who was with you?"

His voice was deep with a slightly gravelly quality that came with age. Combined with the cold, detached look in his eye, it was enough to make my skin crawl every time he uttered a word.

"She's dead," I said quietly.

"Ah, of course. Killed by the plague, no doubt."

I didn't correct him. He didn't deserve to know the truth.

"Just like your sister," he added.

I would almost swear I saw the ends of his lips curl into a hint of a devious smile. Was he taunting me? Trying to get me worked up? If so, it was working.

"What are you doing here?" I demanded.

He tilted his head quizzically as if I should already know.

"The same thing as you, of course." He stepped closer to the glass and lowered his voice. "The Rose Contingency."

A chill ran down my spine as he spoke those words.

"How do you know that name?" I whispered, momentarily short of breath.

He smiled in sadistic amusement. "I know more than you could possibly imagine, Alex. We don't have someone as important as Shayra Lee on our team without keeping a close watch on her life."

"And her death."

"You are referring to the man who was watching her hospital room? Nigel was his name. Poor fellow. Died just a few hours after your sister did."

My fingers involuntarily tightened around the grip of the pistol in my hand. His disconnection from the situation made me sick to my stomach.

"My sister is dead because of you," I said curtly.

"Your sister is dead because of you," he retorted with a sudden aggression in his voice. "As well as every other human on this planet. Including Charlie."

My heart sank at the mention of her name. How could he possibly know who she was?

"How long have you been watching me?" I asked forcefully.

He chuckled. "Let's just say we've always been close by. I don't think you realize just how important your sister was. Her work in genome randomization within polymerase chain reactions became the basis for this entire project."

He motioned to the facility around us.

"Shayra created Project Legion?"

"Not quite. Her work was the basis for it, but she had no knowledge of that. It's better that way. We let our scientists do the leg work, but then we take it from there. The less they know, the less chance there is for the information to find a way into the wrong hands for, shall we say, reasons of conscience."

"So you made them do the work and then you pocketed the money?"

"Money? None of this is about money. It's about the advancement of knowledge. It's about being remembered for something great. And that kind of high calling requires sacrifice."

"Sacrifice?" I fumed. "That sacrifice had a name, and you dragged that name through the dirt by blaming this whole thing on her."

"Well, we couldn't really tell the press the truth, now could we?" I could feel the muscles at the base of my skull tightening as he spoke. "Can you imagine if people had found out that an unqualified, unauthorized simpleton had fiddled with a top secret experiment and caused a plague of this magnitude?"

"You let everyone in the world die thinking my sister was a monster because you were afraid of a little bit of bad PR? Everybody who was a part of the press is dead. What could that possibly matter now?"

An evil looking grin crept across his lips.

"That's the problem with *boys* like you, Alex. You always think too small. You see, but you have no vision."

"Educate me then," I said sarcastically.

"Your sister was a woman with vision. But she lacked the spine to reach greatness. When the nano-organisms began to spread, I already knew there was no saving the human race. But thanks to the letter Shayra left for you on her computer, I saw that there was a way to start over. So, after making the public statement to the press, I came here. This facility runs on a combination of solar power and renewable generators. I have enough non-perishable and freeze dried food items in here to last me three life times. And all I have to do now is wait. Do you see that counter over there?"

He pointed to a box protruding from a computer console on the south side of the room. On it a small digital screen read:

AIR SATURATION: 56%

"That readout tells me the saturation of the nano-organisms that remain in the air. Already that number has dropped three points since I came in here two weeks ago. As the human race dwindles and the remaining animals tear each other apart, the nano-organisms will die. Once that number reaches zero, I can safely emerge and put the plan into action."

I could hear my heartbeat pounding in my ears. An uncontrollable anger was rising in me.

"You let Shayra take the fall for everything," I said through gritted teeth. "For what you created. And now you're going to use *her* plan to try and save the world."

"I wouldn't expect someone like you to understand such things."

"But I do understand. You tied the apocalypse up like a noose and you hung it around my sister's neck, just so you could be the hero of the new human race."

"As I said before, much must be sacrificed in the pursuit of the greater good."

I could feel the rage eating away at logic like a cancer. He deserved to be punished. But there was no science board to which I could report him. There were no authorities to call. There was no one left.

No one except me.

I slowly raised the pistol in my hand until it was pointed at the center of his chest. I guessed it would take a bullet or two to break the glass on the door and then a few more to finish the job.

A scowl crossed his face.

"Who are you kidding, Alex?" he growled. "We both know you're not capable of something like that."

"You don't deserve to live," I said, my voice shaky.

My heart rate accelerated as I steadied my hand and prepared to take my shot. A beeping sound briefly drew my attention to the console to my right. A message flashed across the attached monitor.

Implantation successful. Incubation in progress.

The countdown on the first pod had finished. I would deal with that in a moment. I refused to be distracted from the task at hand. I refocused my eyes on Dr. Gainsborough and aimed my weapon once again at his chest, moving my index finger to rest on the trigger.

This was it. Justice for the human race. Recompense for the ones I had lost. For Shayra. For Charlie. For everyone.

I tightened my grip on the pistol to prepare for the recoil. It was then, for the first time in two weeks, that I heard my sister's voice.

42

"Hello, Allie." Shayra's voice came through the speaker in the ceiling above my head.

Instinctively, I turned my head towards the only screen in the room, the same one that had announced the completion of the implantation process, to see if the message included more than just audio.

Her image filled the computer monitor. She sat in the same hospital bed where I had last seen her alive. She had the same hospital gown on, the same crease in her hair from her recently removed pony tail, even the same eyes, tired, yet alert.

"It's Tuesday, April 20th, 2032," she continued, almost sounding like she was recording some sort of log. "I'm not sure when you will get to see this message, but if you are seeing it, it means you have been successful in implementing my plan. I don't know the exact location of the cloning facility in Oklahoma city, but the Lykos computer systems are all connected, so I was at least able to gain access to that."

I let my arm relax, bringing the pistol to rest at my side. I glanced towards Dr. Gainsborough to see him also riveted by the image on the screen, a look of curiosity and slight annoyance on his face. I turned back to the monitor as Shayra continued.

"I'm setting this video to play on all the screens in the facility as soon as the implantation process on the first pod is complete and incubation is under way."

The business-like demeanor she had been carrying thus far faded and she smiled at the camera and, it felt like, at me.

"It's only been an hour or two since you left my room here at JPS, but by the time you are seeing this, today will probably seem like a distant memory for you. I am sorry that when we spoke I couldn't really tell you the entire truth. If I had, you never would have left my side and I had to have time to prepare for what's coming."

She paused for a moment, collecting her thoughts and, it appeared, her emotions.

"We've always protected each other, you and me. Since we were kids. As long as we were facing it together, nothing really seemed that scary. Like when we first moved to Fort Worth. Remember how you ran and grabbed that knife from the kitchen when the wind blew the screen door open our first night there? We decided to camp out in the living room together, and by the end of the night we couldn't stop laughing about how scared we had been of the wind."

I allowed a smile to form at the corners of my mouth. I did remember.

"But now you are facing the biggest thing that you've ever had to face, and I can't protect you from it. And maybe that's ok. Maybe you never really needed me to protect you. Just like we never really needed protection from that screen door." One side of her mouth curled into a half smile. "I could not be more proud of you, Alex. And not just because I know you'll pull this plan off. I've always been proud to be your sister. You are an amazing man. All you've ever needed was the opportunity to see it."

Her smile disappeared and she looked down towards her lap.

"I'm sorry about Charlie," she said somberly before looking back towards the camera. "I'm sure she's gone by now. You should know that giving up the remainder of her life to be there for you was a task she accepted happily, even after I laid out what exactly it would mean. She said she could think of no better way to spend her life. Actually, I think 'Heck yes.' was how she initially put it."

I let out an involuntary chuckle. I could picture her saying exactly that.

"I can only imagine what you've had to go through to get to where you are now," she continued, "or what sacrifices you may have to make in the future."

I gathered from that statement that she had already come to the same conclusion as Charlie and me about my final part in the survival of the human race.

"But right now, only one thing really matters. You gave the human race a second chance. And I can honestly say, even from this side of things, I never doubted you for a second."

She pursed her lips as tears began to build in her eyes. "I had so much more I wanted to say, but I can't think of any of it right now. Oh well. Maybe I'll remember by the time you get here with lunch tomorrow."

I felt a twinge in my gut. We never got to have that lunch.

"It's a new world you're standing in. A fresh start. Tomorrow truly is a new day."

She smiled once more as a tear finally broke free and rolled down her cheek.

"Goodbye, Alex," she said.

She reached up to wipe the tear away just before her image disappeared and the screen returned to the message announcing a successful implantation.

I stood frozen, attempting to blink away the moisture in my eye and fight back the lump in my throat.

"Goodbye," I whispered back.

I turned back to Dr. Gainsborough who, surprisingly enough, had said nothing through the duration of the video. His expression, however, spoke volumes. A look of pure disgust covered his face.

"Sentimentality never accomplished anything," he hissed.

I ignored him, and instead focused my attention on the glass between us. I had never noticed that Shayra and I had the same eyes until I saw them staring back at me in my own reflection. As her words swirled through my mind, I knew what I had to do.

"We can only start from here," I said out loud.

"What?" he snapped.

"You don't deserve mercy. But Shayra would say I should give it anyway."

"I knew you couldn't actually kill anyone," he said with an arrogant smile.

"No, you're right, I'm not going to kill you. I'm going to tell them what you did."

His smile disappeared, "What?"

"I'm going to write down everything you did. And when the new human race is born, they'll read it. And they will see you for what you really are. And every generation will tell the story to their children, and their grandchildren. And you will forever be remembered as the man who brought this plague on the world."

His disgust turned to rage as I turned to leave.

"Is that your idea of mercy?" he growled at me as I walked away.

I stopped before I reached the door. After a brief moment of thought, I walked back over to the glass that separated us.

"Just in case you get tired of waiting to die in there," I lay the pistol on the tile floor, just outside the safety of the quarantine room door, "here's your mercy."

I turned once again towards the exit, and this time I didn't stop.

43

I immediately returned to the incubation room, first to check on the first two pods, and secondly to resume work on the remaining ninety-eight.

I tried to put Dr. Gainsborough out of my mind. There was nothing I had wanted more than to put an end to his miserable and devious life, but I knew Shayra wouldn't have wanted me to. She would have told me something about how he wasn't worth my mental energy. So, instead I let my thoughts drift to Charlie.

My mind landed on our wedding night. I remembered the way her eyes glistened in the fire light as she recited her vows and the sincerity there as she spoke of a love that finally reached as deep as her pain. In this moment, I finally understood what she meant. In the silence and solitude of my work on these pods, her memory gave me a quiet strength to keep going. Her love created a safe place in my soul that no amount of loss could touch.

Shayra had left her own kind of mark on me as well. The kind that only a big sister's love can make. Her voice was always in my head, urging me onwards. Her influence wouldn't let me give up or stop to focus on mistakes. I remembered the conversation we had the night before her birthday. I could almost see the contrast of blue and orange light and smell the coffee. The last of innumerable cups we had together.

"I believe in you, Allie," she had told me that night. *"I always will."*

And in the end she proved it.

My memories dissipated like a cloud as my concentration shifted to the schematic in my hand. I had found the next pod that was closest to operating condition and had began work by soldering the missing connections on the main logic board. Once I had it in place, I could move on to the cooling system that—

My concentration was shattered by the sound of a thunderous explosion from behind me. A splatter of red liquid covered the pod in front of me as the logic board shattered in my hands. I became instantly aware of a searing pain in my shoulder. My brain rushed to put the pieces together as I instinctively clutched the burning area of my shoulder and fell to the ground.

I had been shot. I rolled painfully to my back to get a look at my assailant.

Dr. Gainsborough stood just inside the door of the incubation area. The gun I had left on the floor outside the quarantine room was in his hand. Smoke from his first shot wafted up from the barrel and disappeared into the air.

"A member of your family has robbed me for the last time," he growled.

I crawled frantically to the other side of the pod, blood dripping through my fingers as I clutched my shoulder.

"We never robbed you. You did this! All of it!" I yelled from behind the pod.

He let out a sinister chuckle that almost made me physically shudder. "Do you know how your father got his job at The New York Post? Did he ever tell you that story?"

My father? What was he talking about? I vaguely remembered him mentioning it. He had cracked some sort of local scandal and it went national.

When The New York Post caught wind of it, they called and offered him a position.

Dr. Gainsborough continued his story without waiting for a response from me. "There was a company known as Wolff Bioinformatics."

As he spoke, he paced back and forth like a tiger, looking for his opening to strike. The lid on the pod was curved so I could make out his shape crossing the room, though slightly distorted through the glass. I made sure the pod remained between myself and his weapon.

"It started as a research lab mainly," he continued, "but over time they discovered the power of genetic technology. Fifteen years ago they started a series of secret experiments to enhance natural capabilities. First in animals, but with a plan to test on human subjects."

He was now making his way down the side of the room, holding the gun lowered at his side as he walked slowly and continued talking. He was waiting for me to let my guard down.

"But before the human tests began, a journalist, your father, found out about the experiments. He went public with the story. Wolff Bioinformatics was disbanded and the scientist who had started the company was arrested. Thankfully, the harshest laws at the time only prohibited genetic manipulation in humans so he was slapped with a fine and released a few weeks later. Unfortunately, his career had already been utterly destroyed. He was forced to start a new company under an assumed name in order to pay off the fines that had been levied against him."

Suddenly it clicked. My dad had in fact told me this story.

"That…that was you?" I asked. "You're Thomas Wolff?"

"Not any more. Officially Thomas Wolff died fifteen years ago. Suicide, I'm afraid. Your father took everything from me. Everything for which I had worked so hard."

He had made his way along the side of the room and was now walking through the pods. I had shifted to the opposite side of my pod from where I had started in order to keep it between us.

"When your sister applied for an internship, I saw an opportunity. She was brilliant. I knew she would make a lot of discoveries for Lykos. But that wasn't the main reason I brought her on. I knew, given enough time, an occasion would present itself. An occasion to ruin his daughter's career the way he ruined mine. And as fortuity would have it, you gave me that occasion."

I stood from behind my pod and took a confrontational step in his direction. "You piece of—"

He raised the pistol and took aim. I immediately dove behind another pod as he fired off four shots. Shards of the pod rained down around me, including the glass from the lid. After the debris settled I heard several benign clicks, followed by rapid foot steps heading towards the door.

He was out of ammo.

I stood once again and followed him out of the room. Just before we reached the storage room door, I threw my entire weight into his back using my right shoulder. We crashed together into the closed door and then fell to the cold tile floor, both of us groaning the entire way down.

I attempted to stand quickly, but the pain in my shoulder and, I assumed, the blood loss from the gunshot wound were starting to affect my vision and motor skills. About the time I had made it halfway to a sitting position, Dr. Gainsborough's hands wrapped around my throat and pulled me up the rest of the way to standing. With a tight hold around my neck, he slammed me head first into the cabinet behind me.

"I will not be remembered as a monster!" he hissed through gritted teeth as his grip around my throat tightened.

I clawed at his hands, trying desperately to break their hold. The edges of my field of view were beginning to darken as my brain fought for the oxygen it needed. I could feel the warm blood dripping from my shoulder, running down my torso and all the way down to—

Leather soled shoes.

I caught a glimpse of the metal bowl and articulating arm I had used to fuse the egg and nucleus of the two completed embryos. The process only required a small electric current, however the machine was capable of a much larger shock.

I had one chance to end this here and now.

With my last remaining vigor, I grabbed the back of his head and slammed his forehead against mine. That seemed to disorient him just enough to loosen his grip. Even though my head was reeling from the impact, I capitalized on the moment and jammed my knee into his stomach. He stepped back and came to rest against the bowl of the device. I did a swift assessment of the situation.

I couldn't use the needle to hold him in place without risking damage to the device. But I also couldn't step away or he would have time to move. I would have to hold him beneath the needle. With my rubber soled shoes, I had a higher chance of survival than he did, but it was still no guarantee. That would have to be good enough.

I reached around him to turn the dial to the maximum level of ten thousand volts before mashing the activation button with all my anger. As an alarm began to sound indicating we had five seconds to clear the area, I grabbed him by the shirt collar and pulled his face close to mine.

"Much must be sacrificed for the greater good," I whispered his words back to him.

His eyes grew wide and he started pulling at my arms. I forced him backwards beneath the needle and into the path of the electric shock as the final alarm sounded. He cried out in pain as the current passed through his body and then traveled into mine. In that moment, as the electricity clenched my muscles, I couldn't have released my grip on him even if I had wanted. My body convulsed involuntarily. My senses began to shutdown as all of them gave way to the unrelenting pain coursing through me.

And then, suddenly, it all stopped. The room went sideways as I fell to the floor. The impact of my head on the concrete left an echo bouncing around in my head. The world started to fade, and as it did, thoughts of Charlie filled my mind's eye. I desperately reached for them, as I had after she pushed me out of the way of that Rottweiler. But the images of her dissolved into a cloud of swirling particles. Then the cloud dissolved into nothing.

44

Friday, May 7th, 2032

I woke up on the floor two days later. To be honest, I didn't expect to wake up at all. As I fell, I had already accepted the fact that I would probably bleed out from the gunshot wound as I lay unconscious on the concrete floor of the lab. As it turned out, the electric shock had somewhat cauterized the wound and mostly stopped it from bleeding.

Dr. Gainsborough, however, was not so fortunate. I found his body devoid of any pulse a couple of feet away from where I had fallen.

Every muscle in my body ached and, at first, I found it difficult to even stand up. But over the course of a few days, I started regaining motor function and even managed to dig a shallow grave to hold Dr. Gainsborough's body. I guess, in the end, everybody deserves something. Although, I buried him in front of the church, as far away from Charlie as I could.

It has been almost one year now since I started writing this account of my story. Almost one year since Shayra and Charlie died. Most of my hours are consumed with working on the remaining pods. So far I have managed to get twenty-five of them working and implanted, and even managed to combine the parts of the two pods that were damaged during Dr. Gainsborough's attack. However, because of the extent of the damage to one of them, there will only be ninety-nine pods that are usable.

It strikes me what an unfair thing it is that Shayra, who conceptualized this plan to save the human race, and Charlie, who gave her life to help me accomplish it won't be here to see it actually become a reality. They deserved this moment far more than I did.

Of course, as it turns out, I won't be here either. The truth is that if I am still alive when you emerge, the nano-organisms will spread to you and the plague will start all over again. To keep that from happening, I will have to die.

I have already found an ample supply of potassium chloride, which is the drug used in lethal injections to stop the heart, and have prepared a syringe containing ten milliliters. According to my research, the affects of such an injection will be quite painful. But if I, and consequently the nano-organisms, are still alive when the remaining time on the first pod reaches three hundred and sixty-five days, I will do what I must.

I'm not sure why the scientists who were heading up Project Legion thought it necessary to keep so much of that particular chemical on hand. I can find no mention of it in any of the notes, but based on what I know of Lykos' code of ethics, I can take a guess. If a clone, or a batch of clones, didn't come out quite right, they would have needed a way to euthanize them. It's no wonder they kept projects like this as much of a secret as they could, even from their most capable and involved employees like Shayra.

I still have dreams about her, but they're different now. No more hospital room and angry accusations. Sometimes it's just a replaying of old memories, like the time we went to Arbuckle, or one of the many times we watched both of the *Titanic* movies to celebrate her birthday. But other times we sit in the dining room of our old apartment and talk over coffee, just like we used to. We talk about the future and what we think it will be like when the new human race begins. She tells me how none of it would have ever been possible without me. I return the sentiment.

I have dreams about Charlie as well. We talk about all kinds of thing. Like what our children would have been like, the hobbies we would have taken up together, or what life would have been like if none of this had ever happened. And then there are times when we say nothing, and I just hold her.

I saved the world. I can say that now. But in the end, was it really me? The more time that passes, the more I realize an important truth about life: Sometimes it's not who you are at all that makes you a hero, but rather it's a matter of who you have in your life.

Without Shayra, I was a thirty-two year old man with no motivation and no ability to keep a job. And yet, in the middle of that, she refused to stop believing in me. She bet the future of everything on me. And I succeeded partly because I didn't have the heart to let her down.

And without Charlie, well, I wouldn't be alive. She stepped out of that quarantine room, knowing full well that she would be dead in forty-eight hours, just so she could be there for me. But as it happened, she didn't hesitate to give her life for me even sooner than that.

So, yeah, I guess I did save the world. But only because they saved me first.

Like I said before, I spend most of my time fixing the pods. But whenever that gets too difficult or monotonous and I need to focus my mind on something else, I work on writing down my story. Well, their story, really.

I have several reasons for putting this account down in writing. First of all, when the human race re-emerges, it will play an important part in helping you to understand what happened to those who came before you. The pods allow for, not only the pre-programming of advanced knowledge such as chemistry and engineering, but a course of basics as well. All the clones will emerge with a knowledge of mathematics, grammar, foreign language, and other subjects, including world history. This history, of course will not include the events that started in April of 2032. This account will hopefully fill in some of the gaps.

Secondly, the world passed into memory thinking my sister was the cause of its destruction. I will make sure those who come after me will know the truth.

And lastly, this information will hopefully serve as a warning and a reminder to those who would try to wield power they can't control. I am not naive enough to think that the new human race will have no bad people, but I will challenge them with this thought that I gleaned from a dear friend that I lost some time ago: You can't stop there from being bad people in the world. All you can do is make sure you're not one of them.

In the end, the past is important. It helps us learn. But the future is infinitely more important than the past. The future is the only place we can cause change. The future is where our choices end up. We can't go back and change the mistakes of the past. We can only start from here.

EPILOGUE

Saturday, May 11th, 2052

The first of us are awake. We have knowledge we can not account for and skills we did not learn. We emerged from what felt like a dream and stepped into a world we did not understand. The information we find in our memory does not match the state of the planet in actuality.

I emerged first, followed soon after by the female. We stepped out of this facility and into the open air, feeling the wind on our face for the first time. But there was no movement. No bustle of people or cars as it was in the the image of everyday life that we had received.

We returned to the facility to see if we could discover answers to the quandaries with which we were confronted. That is where we discovered the body of the man we now know to be Alexander Lee. On the counter next to him we found a syringe, still filled with ten milliliters of liquid. He had made preparations to sacrifice himself in order to stop us from being infected by the plague that had destroyed mankind. However, it seems he instead succumbed to natural causes and his preparations had been in vain.

Clutched in his hand, we found a handwritten note that contained instructions for those of us who would awaken first. Based on the date on the note, we estimate he died approximately two years ago. It took some time to decipher, as the words seem to have been committed to paper when he was in a deeply weakened state.

The first instruction he gave us was pertaining to our names. He said that I was to be named Charles and the female was to be named Shayra, after those whom he called "the heroes of his story." He told us that we could choose our own last names, and so we matched the DNA sample number from the log of the cloning pod to the original sample and adopted the last name of the donor.

The next instruction he gave was in reference to the manuscript you now hold in your hands. He said that all of us should read it, as it would help us to understand the fall of the human race and how this new iteration of mankind came to be.

This story of The Rose Contingency will become a guiding light for our future.

We buried his body among the grove of dragon fruit trees we found behind the church where his wife was also laid to rest. In his note, he said he waited to start the first pod until the second one was ready, so that none of us would have to be alone the way he had been for the last eighteen years. He also said the last of us should emerge approximately five years after the first.

This facility is also equipped with an embryonic storage unit that contains samples which can be used to rebuild parts of the animal life that once resided on this planet. Though, we are fairly certain that was probably not its original purpose. But as it turns out, some of the more resilient species managed to survive, given that the aggressive behavior caused by the plague was temporary and faded as the number of nano-organisms in the air dwindled.

The readout in the quarantine section of the facility now indicates the nano-organisms at an air saturation level of 0%.

As we step out to begin rebuilding our world, we will let the following words guide us as we establish a new society, words we only know to be attributed to one by the name of Anne, who resided in Green Gables: "Tomorrow is a new day, with no mistakes in it."

These words will become the mantra of our new civilization.

Here ends the account of Alexander Hamilton Lee: The man who saved the world.

- *Charles Gainsborough*

ACKNOWLEDGEMENTS

In the summer of 2017, a story idea came to me in the shower. It was not unusual for me to play out a scene or a story fragment in my imagination, but this was altogether different. The pieces of the puzzle fell almost autonomously into place, and as I watched in my minds eye, the themes, the characters, and even their relationships and interactions unfolded before me. I frantically jumped out of the shower and began writing down the bullet points of the story before I forgot.

At first, I had no idea what to do with the story I had created. I had no experience with books, screenplays or any other long-form storytelling medium. But the more I thought about it, the more I was pulled towards the idea of turning the story into a novel. So, a few months later, I sat down at a table at one of our local coffee shops with my laptop and I just started writing.

By the way, if you are looking to try something extravagantly new, the best advice I can give is to just start. There really is no other way around it.

On May 27th, 2018, I typed out the final words of the first draft of The Rose Contingency. Since then it has gone through three and a half years of proofing and rewriting, six drafts (if my count is correct), and countless hands and minds to help it become the story you are holding in your hands. Though it is not my first published work, it is where my writing journey started. Because of that, it will always hold a unique place in my heart and life.

The finished product of this book owes much of its life to the contributions of others, and I would like to give those people their due credit for the part they played in bringing this book to life.

Starting with my first round proofing team: Jill, Sandra, David, Breezy, Virginia (also known to me as MeeMaw), and of course, my mom, who is always one of the biggest supporters of any creative project to which I put my hand.

Thank you to Donna, fellow author and second round proofreader.

In the vein of thanking other authors, I want to give a shout-out to author Jon Acuff. His book *Finish* was the catalyst that I needed to push forward and complete this project. If you are struggling to complete a project, I can't recommend this book enough.

I was out of my depth in a couple of the subjects tackled in this story, and so I had to bring in outside expertise. Firstly, thanks to my dad for being my science consultant. I chose him, not only because he happens to have a masters degree in chemistry, but because he is also one of the most brilliant men I know. Secondly to Kristen, medical consultant and character inspiration (chapters 5 through 7). Thanks for helping make the story more realistic, and also for letting me drop you into the apocalypse.

I think the characters in this story, more so than any others I have yet created or conceptualized, borrow much of their personalities from my children. Whether it's their loyalty to those they love, their hunger to learn and discover, or their fiercely independent spirit, I found inspiration in their souls to create some of my favorite characters to date. Thank you for being you.

Lastly, to my wife Jamie, who believed that The Rose Contingency was going to be a bestseller before I ever even typed the first word. If the world was ending, I wouldn't have to come over. Because I would already be there.

-Colby

Made in the USA
Middletown, DE
18 May 2023

30854017R00229